Villain or Victim is the story of two very different men, each relentlessly pursuing very different lives but both bound for destruction.

The one, David Campbell, a likeable but lonely young man, witnesses his family suffer as a result of the Russian Revolution and the effects of International Communism. The hatred this generates over-rides all patriotic feeling as he watches with horror the tide of war turn and realises that the defeat of Germany at the hands of the Russians will lead in turn to the eventual occupation of all Europe by the Stalinist hordes. Throughout the war he transmits vital information to his country's foes in the belief that stopping Stalin is more important than defeating Hitler.

The other man knows no principles, being driven only by perverted sexual passion and the need to gratify his desire for the power of life and death. Operating in blacked-out Glasgow, he strikes terror into the hearts of a whole community.

Both escape detection, but both die of a broken neck.

VILLAIN OR VICTIM?

A NOVEL BY
Webster Simpson

VILLAIN OR VICTIM?
© WEBSTER SIMPSON 2001

ISBN 0 9538690-2-4

Published by
Itelsor Ltd
Trendell House
3 Lintrathen Street, Dundee DD5 8EF
Tel: 01382 825629 Fax: 01382 832316

INVERNESS

The Great Glen

GRAMPIAN
MOUNTAINS

Glenshee

Blairgowrie

Luss

Loch Lomond

Perth

Helensburgh

Dumbarton
Clydebank

Glasgow

Prologue

The man known as Arthur Donald Nelson paced uneasily up and down the narrow cell.

"What's the time now?" He demanded of the two prison warders who shared the small space with him.

"Eighteen minutes past seven," said one gruffly, consulting his watch. "You won't have long to wait now."

Not long to wait! Forty-two minutes to be precise! How many other men in Britain knew to the minute how much longer they would live? Forty-two minutes. No! More like forty-one now, then he must die at the end of a rope for a crime he had not committed. The seconds ticked by and he reflected on the trial, the case for the prosecution, the damning evidence that had ensured a 'Guilty' verdict, evidence against which he had been able to offer no defence. Then there had been the silly charade of the judge, black cap balanced precariously on his head, pronouncing the death sentence. His appeal had been a formality, doomed to failure. There would be no crowds outside the prison this morning to protest at his execution. No-one in the whole of Britain had a shred of sympathy for him.

Must be less than thirty-five minutes now. His mind went back to Maidstone Crown Court and the unfolding evidence. His counsel had majored on the purely circumstantial nature of the evidence. The defendant listened from the dock. Circumstantial evidence, if there is enough of it and no answer to it, can be very compelling. In all honesty, he thought, were he on the jury, he would have to bring in a 'guilty' verdict. Even he had not realised the strength of the prosecution case in the Crown versus Arthur Donald Nelson. They had, in accordance with the practice of English law, proceeded with only the one murder charge but the other deaths were inevitably obliquely referred to. Arthur Nelson, age thirty-nine, had been interviewed by police in Tunbridge Wells about the sexual assault and murder of three children, the oldest being eight. They had strong suspicions, but not enough to hold him on. Reluctantly, they released him. Then more evidence came to light but, by then, he had completely disappeared. The autumn of 1941 was not the best of times for the police to mount a nation-wide man-hunt. Although less severe than during late 1940, the German bombing offensive was throwing everything into chaos as night after night bombs rained down on London and those towns and cities surrounding the capital. An assortment of vagrants, deserters and others with no good story to account for themselves had been pulled in, but Arthur Donald Nelson had vanished without a trace. It was easy to vanish in war-torn Britain. It was not easy to live, however, without an identity card, work-permit or ration-book.

Nelson had sought temporary refuge in the boarded up, partially demolished sprawling home of his uncle's in Bromley. It had been hit early in the 1940 blitz. The east wing where his aunt and uncle lived took a direct hit, killing them instantly. The shaken remains of the house were not safe for human habitation, but Nelson concealed himself there whilst he contemplated his future. He must get out of the south-east. Fleeing the country was obviously impossible, but somewhere up north he might be able to establish a new identity.

Under cover of the black-out in the late September evening, he made his way to the railway station, but not to catch a train, that was too risky, but to get something to eat and to assess the situation. There were no trains running. The line had been hit twice during the day. A black-board notice optimistically forecast business as usual from 10am the next day. As he read the notice, Nelson noticed a man of much his own age standing beside him and looking rather lost. The fellow turned and spoke.

"Bit of a nuisance this. I've already been delayed by hours. I'd hoped to get the night train from Euston but this puts paid to that. Finding digs at this time of night'll be nigh on impossible. I'm afraid its a bench in the park for me."

"If you don't mind roughing it, I can offer a roof over your head," replied Nelson. "No running water, but no rain either," he went on with a grin. "Slightly better than a bomb-site, but you're welcome if you like."

"Any port in a storm! I've slept in some pretty rum places since 1939, I can tell you! Thanks! Anything's better than a park bench, especially as it does look like rain."

So the two set off in the darkness. Nelson's mind was racing. Chance was throwing him a life-line. If he could borrow the other chap's identity for even forty-eight hours, he could put five hundred miles between himself and pursuit. It was not difficult to remain unseen. The black-out was rigidly enforced and the streets deserted. The two entered the ruined building through a window at the rear. The bomb had brought ceilings down and the pervasive smell of damp plaster and rotting wood hit them. The salvage corps, followed by looters, had stripped out everything of any potential value. However the falling ceiling had concealed the entrance to the cellar and only someone like Nelson who knew there was a cellar could find it. Below ground, it was reasonably dry. Odds and ends of old furniture had been stored down there and the two men were able to make themselves tolerably comfortable. With the door above shut, they could light candles without risking an angry rebuke from an ARP warden or a passing policeman. There was no food but Nelson's uncle had maintained a reasonable wine-cellar before the war. Virtually every bottle was smashed, but they did find some rather good French white wine. Drinking this inelegantly from the bottle, the two exchanged experiences. As the mellowing effect of the wine took hold, Nelson listened with growing interest to the other's tale. He had been in France with the British Expeditionary Force in 1940, only to leave ignominiously with a third of a million others from Dunkirk. The boat that brought them off was hit by bombs. He was wounded and that was the end of the fighting for him. Nelson had noticed that the man did have a slight limp. Like himself, the other had been drafted into munitions production although clearly he, Nelson, was by far the better qualified of the two, having an engineering background.

During the winter bombing offensive, the Germans had wreaked destruction over much of southern England.

One such raid had wiped out the poor fellow's entire family. He himself had only escaped because he was on night-shift. Now he had managed to get himself transferred north on compassionate grounds and was heading for a job in Glasgow. The wine was doing a good job. Surreptitiously, Nelson poured some of his out into the rubble. He needed a clear head. The other was on his second bottle and becoming maudlin. Pretending to hunt for another bottle for himself, Nelson moved behind the other man. He drew out the knife that he had used with such good effect on those snivelling children and slid it up under the man's ribs into his heart, just as the helpful sergeant in the Home Guard had taught him. There was very little blood. Death had been instantaneous. Fellow probably never felt a thing, being so well anaesthetised by alcohol. Blood did not matter anyway. The man's clothes were no use to him. It was the documents that counted. Everything he needed was there. He could use the man's identity, not just for a couple of days, but into the indefinite future. No-one would find this cellar for years and when they did, he would be far, far away. He really had fallen on his feet this time!

. . . .

Back in the cell, the condemned man pulled himself out of the reverie and back to the present. How long now? Thirteen minutes. He sat down, put his head in his hands and waited.

Chapter 1.

To understand why, in 1939, David Campbell saw things in a radically different way from the perspective of virtually every other inhabitant of Britain, it is really necessary to turn the clock back twenty years. Back to the year 1919 and the pleasant and expensive dormitory town of Helensburgh, some fifteen miles from Glasgow. The railway had made it easily accessible from the heart of what was then the second largest city in the land. That proximity to Glasgow, and its magnificent setting on the River Clyde, had made Helensburgh a very fashionable place to live. High up, in a prominent position overlooking the town in the foreground and the widening expanse of the Firth of Clyde beyond, was the home in which David Campbell had been born and in which he had spent his sixteen years of life.

The boy sat slumped over the desk, his body convulsed with silent sobbing. The morning light glinted through the venetian blinds, casting rays of bright light here and there in the unlit room. The doctor had been and gone. There had been nothing for him to do. Nothing, except to write out the death certificates. It seemed impossible that these two, perhaps the dearest people in the world to the youngster, two who had been full of vital life only two days ago, were lying upstairs awaiting the arrival of the undertaker. The cruel influenza epidemic that was sweeping through Europe had claimed them both in a single night.

The world had been torn to shreds by four years of the most horrific slaughter. Then, last year in November, the guns had at last fallen silent. The killing had stopped. The continent of Europe could, it had seemed, at last look forward to years of peace, to an end of sudden death, to recapturing the joys of life that had been eclipsed in that distant August of 1914 by the storm-clouds of war. Then had arisen this new, silent, invisible, insidious killer - the deadly influenza. The weary, malnourished peoples of Europe were an easy prey. Whole families were wiped out overnight. The killer bugs were indiscriminate. Neither youthful strength nor opulence could provide protection. A man might be in the full vigour of youth in the morning and be dead before mid-night.

Now this implacable killer had invaded the pleasant villa in Helensburgh that was home to the Campbell family. Yesterday that family consisted of husband, wife, two sons and one daughter. This morning it was reduced to two sons and a broken-hearted widower who had lost wife and daughter in the same hour shortly after mid-night.

James Campbell was out. Pulling himself together as became the head of the grieving household, he had washed, shaved and dressed and was even now at the undertakers making the arrangements for the joint funeral. James Campbell was an austere figure. He was a leading light in the local parish Church, a town councillor and a hard-working and prosperous business man. The brass-founder's business, started the previous century by his late father, was already prospering when war was declared. The years of conflict had made the demand for all things brass to rocket and the business, together with the associated company in Blairgowrie that was run by James' younger brother, had been extremely profitable. Now the grieving man was left with wealth, but bereft of the two people in the world dearest to him.

At home, he had left his son, David McKay Campbell, a quiet, self-sufficient, sensitive lad of sixteen. The three servants were huddled together sobbing hysterically in the kitchen premises. David was at a desk in the library, alone with his grief. His older brother, Robert John Campbell was in Blairgowrie. Since his return from the trenches of Flanders, Robert had spent most of his time in the Perthshire town of Blairgowrie with his uncle. His working week was taken up with the transition of the Blairgowrie business from munitions to agricultural engineering. His far-sighted uncle predicted a prosperous future for the still relatively new-fangled motor-car and was determined to be a leading player in this field in rural Perthshire. Robert's spare time was largely spent in peaceful solitude in the Grampian Mountains that stretched for mile upon desolate mile to the north of the town. There he found tranquillity. There he started to recuperate from the mental and emotional wounds of France and Flanders. Physically, he had emerged from his two year's soldiering unscathed. The inner man was still suffering, however, and, like so many other young men of his time, the night-mares continued long after the war to end wars was over.

Having made the necessary arrangements with undertaker, registrar and minister, James Campbell made his way to the Post Office. Austere he might be, but he was not insensitive and he thought carefully as he composed the telegram that would bear the day's sad tidings to his older son. That done, he walked home. Barely able to contain his grief, he climbed the stairs and sat by the bed where the woman who had been his wife for the past twenty-four years lay. In the adjacent room, Moraig, his only daughter, who had survived her mother for less than an hour, also lay. He knew he should seek out his younger son and try to give whatever comfort and support he could but he felt he could not keep his own emotions under control. All his life, he had lived in a culture where men were strong and brave and did not reveal their feelings, especially sensitive feelings like grief and sorrow. Somehow, the sheer unexpectedness of his loss seemed to make it harder to bear. For almost exactly two years while Robert was in the army, his father and mother had lived in daily dread of the arrival of a black-bordered telegram. But Robert had returned safe and well. The clouds had lifted and before them lay the happy prospect of many years of peace and prosperity. Then came the influenza. It was cutting down all before it. By the time it had come and gone, its toll on a suffering humanity would exceed all the horrors of the Great Wars casualty lists.

Chapter 2

The funeral was inevitably a miserable affair. There had been so much dying. Scarcely a family had emerged from the War without loss. Some families had sent son after son to die in the Flanders mud. Now it was this terrible scourge, influenza. The officiating minister was drawn and haggard. The undertaker's men looked desperately tired. Neighbours and friends were loyally there in force, but many looked as though they had no more tears to shed.

James Campbell was surrounded by his remaining family. His brother, Joseph and his normally vivacious wife, Maria, were there. Maria was of Russian extraction. Her grand-parents were wealthy landed people from near Petrograd. Her widower father lived and worked in France. She and Joseph had met in Paris three years before the war and, after a whirlwind courtship, had married, to the delight of both families. With them was, of course, Robert, James' older boy. Robert, now in his early twenties, was a tall, strapping man. He looked generally fitter now than when he had returned from the War, but there was a distinct change in him. Some of this could no doubt be accounted for in the normal maturing process that alters a youth of eighteen and makes him a man of twenty-two. However, the change ran deeper than that. The care-free lad had become a lonely, melancholy figure, his face having a rather haunted, far-away look. He had never talked about his War. Whatever had been his experience of its horrors was locked up inside, never to be so much as glimpsed by friend or family. James's younger son, David, in some ways seemed to have coped with the loss better than any of the other members of the family. James thought this strange, for David was the one who had broken down in uncontrollable weeping on the day his mother and sister had died. At the funeral, even in those especially poignant moments at the grave-side, he had been composed.

In the three days since his loss, James had forced himself to look forward into the future. He would send David to join his brother in Blairgowrie. The two would be company for each other and would help one another recover from their bereavement. More importantly, they would be in the generally healthier climate of Perthshire, away from the worst of the wretched bug that was decimating Glasgow and the surrounding towns. James would have to stay. The work at the brass-founders had to go on and he was the one to supervise it. Besides, long hours of tiring toil might help him adapt, although it would never help him accept his loss.

These thoughts were whirling through his head even during the service itself. Planning for the future perhaps helped insulate him from the reality of what was going on around him.

"Dust to dust. Ashes to ashes," intoned the minister. Why do they need to be so brutally realistic in the middle of the funeral service? wondered James. Yes, the deceased body returned to the dust, but did it help the sorrowing relatives to be so harshly reminded of this in the midst of their grief? Mechanically, he took the cord on first Sylvia's and then Moraig's coffin. The token handful of earth was scattered over the mahogany boxes and the funeral party drifted out of the graveyard.

Chapter 3

The next three months were taken up with work interspersed with hill-climbing for the two brothers. At work, they concentrated on the motor-car side of the business. Their uncle had bought one of the early two-cylinder Talbots. It dated from 1909 and had not run since before the War. Together, the two young men stripped it down, repaired and rebuilt it. By the time they were finished they both had a working knowledge of the mechanical parts, even if the magneto and the electrical system remained something of a mystery. It was during this period that David learned to drive and what would become his life-long love affair with the motor-car began. The old Talbot puttered its way up the glens to the north of Blairgowrie and carried the brothers through the spectacular scenery to the snow-clad hills. As the winter moved on into spring, their climbing experience and skills improved steadily. Brilliantly sunny days, with the sun glinting on the snow fields, went some way to raising their spirits.

At Easter, James decided to take a holiday, something he had been unable to do during the long war years. He had promised Sylvia they would go abroad when peace came. Now, although he found it very hard to contemplate a holiday on his own, he had made up his mind to visit America. He had a distant cousin in New York and a standing invitation to stay. It would do his health good and Robert could manage the brass-foundry business in his absence. So Robert was recalled from Blairgowrie and his father set sail on a cargo liner from Greenock.

David was lonely at first, having spent all his working time and most of his leisure time in the company of his older brother. However, he worked happily alongside his uncle and his mechanical and engineering skills developed rapidly. He found he had an inventive flair. When a problem arose, he tossed it around in his mind, sometimes for hours, sometimes for days. Then, quite suddenly, he would seize a pencil and draft out the answer, often totally unorthodox, but almost always practical. Home life with his aunt and uncle was easy-going and happy. Maria was full of life. Being somewhere between his mother's and his sister's age she did in part start to replace both in his life. Never a day went by without his thinking of the two he had lost. The memories now were of happy times and, increasingly, the memory of that terrible night receded.

His love for climbing grew as the spring gave way to summer. He loved his own company and went on increasingly long exploratory expeditions deep into the Grampians. It was on one of these trips he found, quite by accident, a hidden cave. He thought he saw a peregrine falcon swoop down and disappear on the crags above him. Working his way up, he found at one point his path blocked by a solid mass of juniper scrub. He pushed his way through and came across a cleft in the rock. The opening was narrow but inside it opened up to reveal a roomy dry cave. Confident that it was known only to him, he decided to adopt it as an advanced base for future expeditions. Once he had ferried up to it cooking utensils, a primus stove, a sleeping bag and ground-sheet he had a good over-night stopping place and was relieved of the need to carry the usual heavy weight of camping equipment with him.

Chapter 4

It was autumn before James returned from New York. The Helensburgh end of the business had flourished in his absence and both there and at Blairgowrie the post-war boom in business continued healthily. The next year and a half passed. The family were enjoying unprecedented prosperity. The only slight cloud on the horizon was the growing communist threat. Russia, worn out with war and nearly bled to death by an incompetent high command in the Imperial Army, had been swept by the Red revolution in 1917. The Tsar and his family had been captured and, if rumour was to be believed, massacred. The early part of 1921 was marked by communist-inspired rioting in both Italy and Germany. Now the red menace was rearing its head closer to home. Political unrest in Glasgow and the other towns on both banks of the River Clyde had given the English language the word 'Red-Clydeside'. The family's Russian connection through Joseph's wife, Maria, made them all the more aware and anxious as the uneasy political drama, both at home and abroad, progressed. The two brothers were working at Blairgowrie when things came to a head.

Their Aunt Maria's grand-parents on her father's side owned massive estates south-east of Petrograd. Throughout the communist revolution they had been unmolested. Nevertheless, recognising that the red revolution had come to stay, they had systematically transferred what assets they could to Paris and to the care of Maria's father who had made his home there. News from Russia was at best patchy. The country was in a state of chaos, following the conflict between white and red Russians. However, letters did come through. Some were received through the good offices of the French diplomatic service. Another channel was through friends in Finland who still had business contacts with Petrograd. Each communication threw Maria into more gloom. The subject dominated almost every conversation.

"They must get out!" Maria said repeatedly. "They should have left last year."

This was now self-evidently true, but said with all the wisdom of hind-sight. It was understandably hard for the old couple whose family had owned the estates for centuries simply to walk out on the only life they had known, taking with them only what they could carry. True, there was a substantial bank balance awaiting them in Paris and loving family as well. However, optimism had given them a faith that all would eventually come right in Russia if they were patient. Now the reality of the situation had imposed itself on them and getting out would not be easy.

"I must go myself," said Maria. "My father's in too poor health to leave Paris. The old people need someone young and fit to lead them out. I must go!"

When Maria's mind was made up, Joseph, her husband, knew better than to argue.

"If you think you must go, so be it, but I'm coming with you. These are not times for a woman to travel on her own."

Robert chimed in, "Joseph, why don't you and I go? It's not a good idea for Maria to go. I've the army experience and am better able than you if things get difficult. However, I don't speak the language so you'll need to come."

"Your uncle speaks the language so appallingly that the Reds will lock him up for attempting to murder their native tongue," said Maria, laughing despite her anxieties. "I've got to go. Only I can pass as a local and can hope to get in and out without attracting attention.

"You're not going without me," declared her husband in a tone that discouraged further argument.

"And neither of you are going without me," said Robert.

"And what about me?" asked David. "Am I to be left out of all the fun?"

"Someone has to stay and look after the business. You're perfectly capable and it will do your status with the staff no harm if we leave you in charge," his uncle replied.

So it was agreed. As time was supremely important, telegrams were hastily composed and despatched. James, in Helensburgh, was told, rather than consulted, about their plans. A ship was departing from Dundee for Helsinki in Finland. From there it would be possible to find a vessel to take them to Petrograd, even if they had to charter a fishing boat.

Chapter 5

David took the train back to Helensburgh that week-end. He
found his father in a deeply depressed state. He had a terrible
sense of foreboding and father and son anxiously awaited
news from the Baltic. It was Tuesday when a terse telegram
confirmed that Joseph, Maria and Robert had arrived in
Helsinki and that a letter was following. By the time the letter
arrived David had returned to Blairgowrie. Once he became
accustomed to the silent house, he adjusted to his solitary
existence. During the day the cook, who doubled as house-
keeper, supervised the maid and the gardener. David's meals
were always waiting for him when he returned from work.
Almost every evening he went back to the engineering shop
and worked on alone. By the time he returned in the late
evening it was to an empty house and a supper laid out ready
for him. Whilst he missed the to and fro of family
conversation, he was not unhappy to be alone. Well-meaning
neighbours and friends of his uncle and aunt would invite him
for Sunday lunch or, occasionally, for supper. He put on a
cheerful face but, all in all, he would have preferred solitude.

James sent on the Helsinki letter. The voyage out
across the North Sea had been uneventful. The winter ice had
cleared from the Baltic and shipping was moving freely. The

three had been able to book places on a small cargo vessel for the short crossing to Petrograd. Communication from Russia itself was likely to be difficult, if not impossible, so James and David were not to worry if there were no word for three or four weeks. As soon as the trio had rescued Maria's grandparents and were safe in Helsinki a telegram would be sent.

There was nothing to do but to wait. Two weeks went by, then three. Still no word. As the fourth week ran on into the fifth, both father and son became increasingly anxious. At the sixth week, James wrote to the Foreign Office. Diplomatic relations with the Revolutionary Government were officially restored, but, in practice, the level of co-operation varied tremendously from place to place. Petrograd was still in a state of turmoil following a mutiny in the nearby naval base at Kronstadt. The Moscow Government under Lenin was nominally in control but unrest among the near-starving populace was a constant threat. When news at last came it was not good. The three from Scotland had reached Maria's family home, persuaded the old folk to leave and returned to Petrograd. There the trail ran cold. The week-end they had arrived had been marked by rioting, looting and considerable loss of life. It did not look good.

James passed on the news to David. David, sensing from his father's brief accompanying note that the older man was nearly out of his mind with worry, hastened to Helensburgh by train. Then all they could do was wait. At last there was news, but news of the very worst sort. The party of five had been caught up in the massive street battle in

Petrograd and had perished. Details were very sketchy, perhaps mercifully so. The delay had been partly to ensure accurate identification and, alas, there was no room for doubt. All five were gone.

James sat holding the Foreign Office letter like a man transfixed. David, having taken in the gist of it, fled to his room and sobbed. Half an hour later, he returned to the library where his father sat exactly as he had been thirty minutes earlier. David spoke, but the older man neither replied nor moved. His son seized his arm. To his horror, he realised that his father had suffered some kind of seizure. He dashed from the room. In the kitchen, the gardener was drinking a cup of tea.

"Quick, man! Get the doctor! Mr James has been taken badly. Quick! Get him here as fast as you can."

The doctor arrived some twenty minutes later. After examining the patient thoroughly, he said, "A stroke. He's obviously had some kind of shock that's brought it on. We'll get him into the nursing home. In cases like this it's very difficult to predict the outcome. If he doesn't have a second attack, there will be some measure of recovery. How much, I can't say. I must be brutally honest with you and say that it's unlikely that he'll totally recover. He may have to learn to speak all over again. Some memory loss is inevitable. He's paralysed down the right side, but that may pass. I'll arrange an ambulance and get him in as quickly as possible."

So saying, he left, leaving David in a state of shock. Was all his family to be taken from him? A man could only stand so much. Five out of six of those close to him were gone. Was he now to lose his father too? Or would his father be left so impaired that he would be better dead?

The ambulance came and went. The young man sat down in the half-lit room and wept.

Chapter 6

The next few days were a living nightmare for David. Every day he visited his father. The older man was improving but his speech was incoherent and slurred. Mercifully, the paralysis ebbed away and he was walking, albeit shakily, but he was walking. His memory was patchy. Some things, particularly from the more distant past, he remembered clearly. However, all recollection of his tragic losses was gone. Why did Sylvia not visit him? Where were Moraig and Robert? Why was it only David who called each day?

Mindful of the need to protect his father from further shock, David evaded the questions as best he could. He realised that he could not go doing this indefinitely and worried about how to bring James back to his real family situation. In the short term, he avoided the problem by having a full agenda of business matters to discuss at each visit. The business side of James' brain seemed least affected and, although he struggled with words and pronunciation, he could conduct a reasonable conversation. However, it always ended with the queries about his wife, his daughter, his other son and, sometimes, his brother.

David dealt with his own grief in his usual way. He worked anything up to an eighteen hour day. When he did go to bed, sheer exhaustion meant he slept reasonably well for four or five hours. After that, sleep was tortured by nightmares. He was in Petrograd. At the other end of a long street, he saw his uncle, his aunt and his brother coming towards him. They waved, they shouted and he started to run to meet them. Then out of a side-street poured a mob, screaming, singing and shouting. They did not seem to see him at all, but they engulfed the other three and the two frail old people with them. What followed varied from one dream to the next. Sometimes he saw nothing, save the backs of those on the fringe of the mob. Sometimes he saw the body of one or other of his relatives flung up in the air. Despite the mad screaming of the crowd, he always heard Maria, in particular, crying out to him to save her. Some times the mob dispersed and he was left alone with barely recognisable mutilated corpses. Always, he woke up trembling and drenched in sweat.

As James' health improved and his thought and speech became more coherent and rational, David found it harder and harder to visit. Sooner or later the evasions would have to stop. What then? Would he tell the truth and perhaps watch his father suffer another, and possibly final, seizure? Mercifully, he did not have to take any decision. One evening he went to where his father was sitting alone in a chair. James turned to him with his eyes welling with tears.

"They're all gone, aren't they?" He asked. "I was sitting on the veranda thinking, and suddenly it was like a door in my mind opening up again. Sylvia and Moraig, dead these past three years? Now Robert, Joe and Maria?" David nodded mutely. James went on, "I kept hoping it was only a dream, but I knew it wasn't."

A long silence followed. A tear ran down the father's cheek but he did not seem to notice it. His son sat beside him, neither moving nor speaking. Once or twice, he opened his mouth to try to say something, but he was too choked up and no words came out. At last the older man broke the silence.

"We'll have to learn to soldier on without them," he said, with a visible effort. "I must get myself better as fast as I can so I can come and help you. From what you've told me, you're making a good job of running things and, in future, I may well have to leave much more of the directing of the business to you. Perhaps we should sell the Blairgowrie end. What do think?"

David found himself strangely reluctant to do so. It did make sense for the two to concentrate on the one business. Whilst both businesses were highly profitable, the capital released from the sale of Blairgowrie would fund expansion in the brass foundry. The brass foundry was situated at Dumbarton, eight miles from the family home at Helensburgh. The rail service between the two towns was excellent which was why, when David's grandfather, John McKay Campbell, had started to prosper, he had moved his family from Dumbarton to the already fashionable and pleasant town of Helensburgh. When his son, James, David's father, thought the time had come to make the business a limited company, he coined the name 'Jayemcee' from his father's initials. The nearby shipyards on both banks of the River Clyde had an insatiable demand for brass fittings of every kind and Jayemcee Brassfoundry was ideally placed to supply these needs.

David thought long and hard about disposing of the Blairgowrie end of the business. There was sound sense to the proposal, but selling Blairgowrie went against the grain. He had enjoyed working there. The staff were as rough and ready as any other engineers and mechanics but they respected him. In the recent weeks, they had co-operated willingly and well, taking orders from him though he was less than half the age of most of them. In the anxious days of waiting, when all had known that both father and son were preoccupied with what was or might be happening in Petrograd, they had worked loyally, even though supervision was almost non-existent. Selling up seemed like selling them down the river. Besides, more selfishly, abandoning Blairgowrie would mean losing the frequent opportunities for enjoying the unfettered freedom of the Grampians.

"Let's wait until you're better and talk again then," he said eventually. "Tom McBain's made an excellent job of being foreman at Blairgowrie. We can make him works manager and, if I go there every week for a day or two, I'm sure he'll more than cope with the extra responsibility. Besides, the Dumbarton plant may not always be so busy. All the ship-builders are working flat out at present, but that's to meet the demand following the losses of ships in the War. When the ships sunk by submarines have all been replaced, there may well be a slump in demand. Blairgowrie is building up the motor transport side, both cars and lorries. That's the thing of the future. There'll be a steady demand on the steam-wagon and traction engine maintenance side for years to come, but alongside it will be a growth in petrol and oil engined vehicles."

So the two decided to make no radical changes in the short term. David travelled frequently between the two businesses, usually managing to spend his week-ends in the solitude of the hills.

Eventually, death certificates acceptable to the Scottish legal system were received via the British consulate in Petrograd and the depressing matter of disposing of the personal belongings of Joseph, Maria and Robert was completed. In the absence of any children, Joseph's will left everything to his brother. James, after much discussion with David, decided to sell the house in Blairgowrie. He made over the proceeds to David who bought a small bungalow on the outskirts of the town.

Although James had made a remarkable recovery, his former confident bearing never returned. His speech was almost perfect, with just a slight hesitancy that had not been there before the stroke. He walked with a stick, but a stranger would hardly notice that he dragged his leg slightly. What had changed was his personality. His decisiveness was gone. He left all decision-making to David. He seldom smiled and often slipped into a black depression. He only went out when he had to. David watched with sadness the tragic change in the character of the father he loved. The only alleviating factor was that their shared sorrows had definitely drawn the two men closer together. In childhood, David had almost feared his aloof and distant father. There was never any demonstration of affection in the family circle. It was assumed that the children knew they were loved and wanted but, neither by word or gesture, was this ever expressed. The distance between them seemed to grow as David matured. At the time of his mother's death father and son lived in the same house like two strangers, always respectful and courteous, but never intimate and affectionate. The hours spent together as David helped his father fight back after the stroke changed that and, for the first time in his life, David found he could confide in someone.

Outside the home, David had many acquaintances, but virtually no friends. His relationship with his staff was friendly, but, with the possible exception of one man, there were none among them to whom he felt he could really open up. That one was James (Jimmy) McDuff, a fellow some seven years older than David, a competent engineer and a man of sufficient tact to be able to speak his mind without showing disrespect. It was to Jimmy McDuff that David increasingly turned for intelligent conversation about the baffling world of national politics and international affairs.

Chapter 7

Towards the end of the year, there was one more event that had a very disturbing effect on David. It so happened that he was at St Enoch's railway station in Glasgow when he heard the raucous singing of the 'Red Flag'. He remembered well the same tune sung to a gentle rhythm by his mother, the hymn tune 'Carlisle'. Now, hi-jacked by the communists and sung to an alien, aggressive rhythm, the raucous words rang round the station platforms. It transpired that the new Member of Parliament, James Maxton, was boarding the train for London to take up his seat there along with Willie Gallagher from Fife, an avowed communist. Unwillingly, and only because he was trapped by the crowd, David listened to an impromptu speech from the newly elected Maxton. To his amazement and his horror, it contained the promise that 'all the railways will belong to the people when we come back.'

Back in Dumbarton, David described the experience to Jimmy McDuff. "They're bragging that they'll be taking over the railways. That'll only be the start, you mark my words! The next thing is that they'll be confiscating factories and mills the length and breadth of the land. It's the slippery slope to national ruin!"

"Do you not think there's a lot of hot air, but, when it really comes to the bit, good old British common-sense will prevail? These hot-heads shout a lot, but it's not the British way to change things by violent revolution."

"I only hope you're right. What we need is someone strong enough in government to stop all this nonsense."

"Well! One consolation seems to be the change in the situation in Italy. That man Mussolini! He's implacably opposed to communism and seems to be getting a real grip on things there."

"Yes," said David. "I'd never heard of him until recently but I'm glad that some one who understands the red menace has achieved a position of power."

"Germany is in a right mess," went on Jimmy. "The communists are still increasing in influence, much of it orchestrated from Moscow. The risk is that it sweeps westwards"

Maxton's words burned their way into David's brain. If the railways were to be taken over by the 'People', would factories like his own follow? Throughout the following year David studied the news reports from both home and abroad. In Germany, the currency collapsed completely, with inflation running amok. The German mark depreciated a billion-fold in the year. An attempted coup led by some unknown called Hitler was put down and the ring-leaders were jailed. The red menace, however, remained.

It was round about this time that David came into contact with others in Perthshire who were alive to the impending danger. He was invited to a shooting party at one of the smaller sporting estates. Never having so much as held a gun in his life, his first instinctive reaction was to decline politely. However, the invitation came through one of the Blairgowrie customers, an influential figure who already owned three cars and several other vehicles. In short, he was too important a customer to risk offending. Besides, he might well be a useful means of making contact with the increasing number of wealthy car-owning Perthshire land-owners.

When he mentioned the invitation to Tom McBain, the garage manager, McBain said, "If you'll excuse me saying so, sir, do you not think you should have a better car if you're to be hob-nobbing with the landed gentry? You know, so that it'll look as though you can really be trusted to look after the maintenance of their vehicles. Yon Talbot's getting too long in the tooth, if you'll pardon me being so blunt."

"Aye! Right enough! The old girl is long past her best. And, of course, you right! I must look as though I really appreciate good cars."

"We're supplying Lord Fotheringham with a new Lanchester next week. His old Rolls Royce might be just the thing for you. Mind you, it's all of ten years old but, it doesn't really look it."

"That's because Fotheringham had it back at the coachbuilders for a new touring body a couple of years ago. It looks bang up to date and the chassis may be pre-war but it's essentially the same as the current model."

"Aye," replied McBain, "Only a real expert would be able to guess its age. I'm sure it's the car for you."

So, a fortnight later, David was a Rolls Royce owner.

The car was incredible! David was delighted that circumstances had virtually forced his hand. It did, of course, have a gear-box, and a very pleasant one at that, but it would start off uncomplainingly in top gear and pull away silently and smoothly to a top speed in excess of sixty miles per hour. The massive forty horse-power engine was as smooth as silk, pulling the car effortlessly up the steep glen roads like a steam engine. It used petrol. Can after can had to be poured in to fill its huge tank. Careful driving might result in fifteen miles from each gallon. Fast driving could easily halve that. The sheer pleasure of driving such a machine more than made up for any disadvantages and, however much a bore the shooting week-end might be, David was sure that he had bought the right car for him.

The week-end was something of a disaster. The other guests seemed intent only on killing things. Anything that flew in the air or that scampered through the heather was at risk. David did take one or two rather tentative shots at grouse, but as none of them obligingly flew into the shot, his bag at the end of the day was nil. As a conversationalist, he was a miserable failure. The only subjects he felt comfortable with, such as motor-cars and their engines, all things mechanical and hill-climbing, were clearly not the talk of Perthshire dinner tables or lounges. There was, in fact, only one guest he really had some affinity for. This man, one Archibald Ramsay, clearly shared his own views on the dangers of communism. The two spent a lot of time in earnest conversation and, as they parted, Ramsay promised to introduce David to others who were of a like mind. That was the only part of the week-end David really enjoyed. His host and hostess probably shared his disappointment. Certainly, whilst he retained their business custom, the invitation to a shooting party was never repeated.

Chapter 8

Archibald Ramsay did keep in touch. David was invited to various political meetings. Sometimes he went. More often he did not. He had managed to cut down his working hours without experiencing any emotional problems. However, he was much happier spending his leisure alone on the hills than in seeking companionship. One man he did meet at this time was to have a profound influence on him. Stephen Myers was a much-travelled business man. Like David, he had engineering interests. The two were soon deep in conversation.

"I believe that you, like myself, have engineering interests?" asked David.

"Yes, indeed. More on the sales rather than the production side. Before the Russian revolution we had had a thriving market in the Tsar's Russia. All that has, of course, changed," replied Myers ruefully.

"But you're still selling in Europe, I understand?"

"Aye! very much so! Our markets are now confined to Western Europe. Mind you, that involves quite enough travel for me! We do business all over the Continent and my travels take me to virtually every capital city and not a few other besides."

"Fascinating," relied David. "You must be uniquely well placed to see how things have developed since the War"

"Fascinating indeed, but also deeply worrying."

"How so?"

"Everywhere there is reason to fear that there's a hidden communist conspiracy. Moscow makes no secret of its intention that communism should replace capitalism throughout the world and its tentacles seem to reach most countries. Even in those with apparently neither an active labour movement nor political freedom, communist agents are stirring up unrest."

"And that includes Britain?" asked David.

"Indeed it does! And yet Britain is blissfully unaware of the potential danger of the enemy in its midst. It's all very disturbing."

"Aye! and we seem powerless to do anything about it."

"Clydeside is a hot-bed of unrest. There are political activists, of varying shades from pale pink to deep red, haranguing crowds at street meetings. Now that the post-war boom is over and the grim reality of unemployment is hitting the ship-yards there is a growing climate of discontent."

"Too true," replied David. "And there are agitators there to take advantage of the situation. It's tough going in engineering nowadays. My own business, Jayemcee Brassfoundry has had to pay off staff, just like almost every other manufacturing business on the Clyde."

"I can't say I'm surprised. Some of the ship-builders have had to slim down their work-force by half in less than a year. It's hardly surprising you're finding things difficult."

"The one consolation is the strength of the Blairgowrie business. The farming fraternity there, always cautious, cling to their ageing, steam-driven traction engines and these need constant maintenance so we've steady enough work."

"And the car side? I imagine that will be hit by the recession too?"

"Not as much as you might think," said David. "The proprietors of the large estates, however, seem to be insulated from recession and the number of private cars in the county is increasing by leaps and bounds. Furthermore, there are also an increasing number of commercial vehicles. Most are ex-military, sold off cheaply as the size of the army has been shrinking following the Armistice. All need regular maintenance and so the hard times are scarcely felt in the Blairgowrie end of the business."

"You'll just need to develop another transport maintenance and garage services business here in Dumbarton."

"You're a mind-reader!" said David with a grin. "That's just what I intend to do."

- - - - - - - - - - - - -

Shortly after this conversation there came another turning point in David's life. His father, James, had been in central Glasgow, visiting the Company's auditors. He was making his way to the railway station through the busy city streets when he was caught up in a noisy political demonstration. There was much pushing and shoving, nothing vicious, but no place for one unsteady on his feet. He was jostled from behind. He missed his footing on the kerb. He fell and smashed his head on the granite.

An ambulance was called. James was hurried to Glasgow Royal Infirmary. David was sent for, but he was in Blairgowrie. By the time he received the telegram it was already late evening. Rather than struggle with trains and train timetables, he jumped into the Rolls and sped off into the darkness. At times he was covering nearly a mile a minute, racing through the night. At just after mid-night he arrived at the hospital, but he was too late. His father had died an hour earlier without regaining consciousness.

The police were helpful and sympathetic. A report was duly sent to the Procurator Fiscal, the Scottish equivalent of a public prosecutor. The Fiscal decided that the circumstances indicated an unfortunate accident. No crime had been committed and the case would be closed. David was furious. Though normally an essentially fair-minded man, he was in no mood to see reason in this matter. His father had been pushed. That push was an assault. The assault led directly to James' death. At the very least, thought David, someone should stand trial for manslaughter. Indeed, if he had his way, the charge would have been murder. However, no amount of arguing, of reasoning, of threatening, of lobbying, altered the fact. The case was closed.

With a deep sense of grievance, David organised the funeral. James had been an important and a respected figure in the community and this was reflected in the attendance at the grave-side. The funeral service was not taken by the same lugubrious minister who had presided at his mother's and his sister's funerals. Instead, a kindly man in late middle age who had served as an army chaplain presided.

"The Lord gave and the Lord hath taken away." The words, wafting over the open grave, riled David. Was the Lord then a party to the death of his father? 'The communists hath taken away!' Now that he could understand. But that was what everyone seemed to want to play down. However, the truth was that the communists had robbed him of everyone he held dear.

Later that evening the clergyman came to visit him. David would have been more than happy to have been left alone, but courtesy demanded that he entertain and listen with patient silence to the counsel of the older man. Rather unwillingly, he found himself articulating the bitter thoughts that had so occupied his mind in the graveyard.

"The communist's have ruined my family," he exclaimed. "You know how they murdered my brother, my uncle, his wife and her parents? Now they've taken my father too. They're even responsible for the deaths of my mother and my sister. Do you wonder I'm bitter?"

"I can't say I'm surprised, but I must say it worries me. How can you blame the communists for the deaths of your mother and sister. That was surely influenza?"

"Aye! That's what carried them off, right enough. But if the communists hadn't inspired the Russian revolution and overthrown the Czar, the Germans would have been defeated in 1917. Instead the communists made a separate peace with the Huns and abandoned Russia's western allies. The result was that the war dragged on and the population of Europe nearly starved. Is it any wonder that the consequences of the influenza plague were so terrible?"

"I think you're perhaps being a bit too hard on the Russians. They'd suffered terribly and were incapable of continuing fighting for much longer."

"It wouldn't have lasted for more than a few more months. If the war had ended in 1917, food production would have been back to normal. Remember! Starvation was a major ally of the flu bug. Not only would my family still be alive, but countless other needless deaths would have been prevented."

"Aye! David! I can understand something of what you feel. But let me say this. Do try to forgive what has happened in the past."

"Forgive? You expect me to forgive? What a thing to ask a man! They've wiped out my family and you say I should forgive!"

"David. Let me speak very frankly to you. You've suffered so much. These past few years have been incredibly hard for you. But you have a life ahead of you. If you face it embittered, you'll be miserable all your days. If you harbour evil thoughts against others it'll be like a cancer growing inside you. One day it'll destroy you."

"I can't forgive! I will not forgive! I'll fight communism until my dying day!"

"David, laddie! I'm scared for you. Please think over

what I've tried to say. I know it's desperately hard, but try to let go of the past. Don't let it ruin your future happiness."

"You're asking the impossible! I cannot and I will not forgive and that's that!"

Chapter 9

The third day after his father's funeral was David's twenty-second birthday. He celebrated it alone. There was simply no one left to share it with. At twenty-two he was on his own, a wealthy young man with two businesses, both still relatively prosperous even in the worsening economic climate. If he felt at all lonely, he did not admit it, not even to himself. In the stillness, he took three decisions. First, he would work, and work hard, to consolidate all his father, his grandfather, his uncle and his brother had put into the business. Second he would remain in the family home in Helensburgh. True, it was ridiculously large for his simple needs, but it was home and selling it was almost like a betrayal of his late parents. Third, as soon as possible, he would visit America.

He had a standing invitation to visit his father's New York friends. Indeed, James had urged him to go. It would widen his horizons, he had said. It was not because David felt a need for wider horizons that he would go. It was simply the realism that the red menace was creeping west-ward. America, that great bastion of capitalism, would stem the red tide. But Britain, still wearied from four years of debilitating slaughter, no longer had the stomach for any kind of fight. David would secure his own position by setting up investment trusts in the United States. If Britain did fall to Lenin's successors, Stalin and his henchmen, there would be the possibility of a new life for David Campbell in the New World.

These decisions behind him, David flung himself into his work with characteristic energy. Not only did he have great natural mechanical aptitude, he had a rare gift for understanding people. His privileged background may have insulated him from the raw poverty that was the lot of the working classes in the early 20th century, but it did not prevent his understanding their essential characteristics and what motivated them. He knew how to draw the best out of them, when to promote and when to dismiss. The choice of Tom McBain to take charge of production at Blairgowrie had been amply vindicated. If David was a frequent visitor at the Blairgowrie plant, it had less to do with commercial necessity and more to do with the pull of the Grampian Mountains. A series of similar wise choices put the various departments of the main factory at Dumbarton in the hands of a reliable team, making the prospect of the American trip a viable proposition.

In the event, the timing of the American visit was determined by the unforeseeable fact that Maria's father in Paris suffered a heart attack and died. His health had not been good all the time that David could remember, but his abrupt departure from this life still came as a shock. He was the last link David had had with the older generation and was, indeed, the only remaining person he had regarded as 'family'. A French firm of lawyers handled the dead man's affairs and they made all the funeral arrangements. This was just as well, for, move as fast as he could, it was a race for David to get to Paris in time for the funeral. There he felt quite out of place, knowing no one. He was the last remaining relative of the deceased, yet he scarcely had known him. His embarrassment was heightened by the evident fact that many other mourners knew his aunt's father so much better than he had done. They were lavish with their sympathy, although he felt that, were the truth told, many of them felt the pain and loss of bereavement more than he did. His discomfort was only increased when he discovered that Maria's father had, after one or two minor bequests, named him as heir.

David left the disposal of the estate in the hands of the lawyers and returned to Scotland. He would have to visit Paris again and so decided to tie this in with the American trip. After an interchange of letters and telegrams with both Paris and New York everything was arranged. His route would be Glasgow to London; London to Paris; Paris to Cherbourg then Cherbourg to New York. All being well he would return within six weeks.

Chapter 10

The first great surprise came in Paris. He had vaguely realised that Maria's family had wealth but was also aware that much had been lost in the aftermath of the Russian Communist Revolution. Much indeed had been lost, but what had been squirreled away in France, added to Maria's father's own personal fortune amounted to a very substantial sum. David, already a rich young man, was now a very rich young man. Some of his inheritance was worthless. He looked with a wry smile at title deeds he could not read because they were in Russian. The lawyer explained that these gave him title to tracts of land south-east of Petrograd amounting to about half the size of Wales! However, there were also investments in businesses on both sides of the Atlantic. David concluded that the shrewd son, each time he received the wealth in various forms when his parents had managed to smuggle it out of Russia, had hedged his bets by making sure that, if Europe fell to the Reds, the family would not be destitute. David found this a comforting confirmation of the wisdom of his own financial planning.

In addition to the abundant wealth represented by paper - share certificates, title deeds, bonds and the like, there was also a significant quantity of jewellery. David was out of his depth with such treasures. He had neither interest in, nor knowledge of, gold, silver and precious stones. To his untutored eye, they all looked priceless. Having no need for further money, he decided that the best course of action was to take them to New York and store them in a safety deposit box there. Should, perish the thought, Sterling suddenly nose-dive in value as had the German currency, such an investment would more than hold its value.

Not surprisingly, David was somewhat apprehensive about crossing the Atlantic with what was by anyone's standards, a considerable fortune in jewellery and cash. However, arguing that as no-one knew he had it, he was at no greater risk than any of the thousands of others who, each year, took ship for New York. The crossing was pleasantly uneventful. The weather was remarkably good, considering it was so early in the year, and he enjoyed every minute of the voyage. The first few days were taken up with making the necessary business arrangements to ensure his investments were in safe hands. Then he was free to sight-see. He did visit some of the obvious attractions that America's leading city had to offer, but he spent far more time visiting its industry. What he saw impressed him greatly. The Americans were far ahead of Britain in their production methods. They invested much more in efficient means of production. They took work-study very seriously. They paid their workers more. They demanded, and got, more from their workers. For David, it was an eye-opener.

The news from Britain was unsettling. The miners were at odds with the colliery owners. There was unrest everywhere. However, in America, the people seemed to work hard and to prosper. Knowing he had more capital behind him than ever, David vowed to re-equip his factories with the best plant he could find, to cut down the number he employed, and to pay those who were left much more than his competitors did. That, he felt sure, was the way forward. By the middle of April, he was home-ward bound for Scotland with a crusading zeal to put Jayemcee Brassfoundry right at the fore-front of enlightened British industry.

Chapter 11

During the weeks David had been away, there had been significant changes in the industrial atmosphere in Britain. The miners had been locked out by their employers. There was talk of a general strike. At street corners, in city squares, at factory gates up and down the country there were agitators. Crowds marched to the singing of The Red Flag. The battle-lines for a major show-down seemed to be being drawn. How different things were in Italy! The new Premier, Benito Mussolini, had outlawed strikes. The notoriously unreliable Italian railway at last had its trains running on time. Meanwhile, Britain, with unrest in every town and city, had a vacillating government and looked as if it were slipping back into an industrial dark-age.

The Trades Union Congress called a general strike in support of the miners and, eight days after his return to Helensburgh, David watched impotently as the mighty Clydeside ship-building industry fell silent. His own staff was on strike. There was no personal animosity about it. They could not have continued to work even if they wanted to. The strike on the whole of the River Clyde was solid. However, David, far-sighted as ever, made it clear that there would be no reprisals. The strike would end. It had to end sometime, and whatever the respective gains and losses might be, workers and management one day would have to co-operate or starve. The strike lasted nine days. By the time the Unions called it off unconditionally, a tremendous amount of damage had been done to industrial relations. Not so, however, in Jayemcee Brassfoundry. By raising wages and re-equipping over the next nine months, David was able to capitalise on the work-force's uncertainty. He managed to boost sales and production to the point that the redundancies he had prepared himself for were unnecessary. The business, both in Dumbarton and Blairgowrie continued to prosper. David had a secure income and his staff had secure jobs.

All this was to be tested to the extreme in the years that followed. As the great slump hit first America and then every industrialised nation, the late twenties and early thirties were difficult years. Companies of many years' standing collapsed. Unemployment soared. Jayemcee Brassfoundry also suffered, but came through the whole experience relatively unscathed.

Chapter 12

David's business progress was not matched by the development of his social life. He did join the local Chamber of Commerce and did, from time to time, attend its meetings and social functions. He became quite adept at using such occasions to secure introductions to individuals whose acquaintance would prove helpful in the business sphere. Howeve, on the merely social front, he was a flop. Apart from being able to talk intelligently and enthusiastically about motor-cars and transport in general, he was a disaster as a conversationalist. He knew better than to bore people with his strongly-held political views. The end result was that, because of his unwillingness to insist on having his own opinions heard, he was considered a good listener and, paradoxically, many thought him wise and did seek his opinions on the subjects that interested them.

Apart from his cars, he did not advertise his wealth. The Rolls gave way to a succession of exotic and fast cars. Lancia, Bentley, Delage, Cadalac, Armstrong Siddeley, Lanchester, one by one they came and went. Each had its own attraction, each its own vices. Each brought satisfaction in its own way. The secret cave in the Grampians had been replaced by a cottage. Built for a shepherd or a game-keeper, the small two-roomed cottage was somewhat more comfortable even though it lacked much in the way of basic services. Water was piped from a near-by stream and both the pipe and, sometimes in extreme weather, the stream itself were liable to freeze up. There was no electricity and only a dry toilet round the back. However, he loved it and he loved the solitude. Once in a while, he would climb the mountains in the company of a like-minded friend. More often he travelled alone.

Despite his Spartan life-style, the mothers of marriageable maidens scented his wealth and, from time to time, he found himself invited to supper. It was amazing to see how often on these occasions, circumstances were so contrived to leave him alone in the company of some young woman who was either as vapid and garrulous as her mother or, like himself, was writhing with embarrassment. When the mothers started gently enquiring how many rooms the Helensburgh villa had or remarked on what a lovely family

home it was, he knew it was time to back off. Different people cope with bereavement, grief and tragedy in different ways. Not for David a 'better to have loved and lost, than never to have loved at all' attitude. Rather, his sorrows led to the development of a hard, protective shell being built up around him. Loved ones were hostages to fortune. Their loss was so awful that he would never again hazard his emotions by letting anyone get really close to him.

The last time he had been in church was at his father's funeral. The minister did visit his home from time to time but the two seemed to live on different planets and David was not disappointed when such calls tailed off.

For all that the resentment he felt for left-wing politicians and communists in particular smouldered away inside him, David was not really a political animal. Archibald Ramsay was a frequent speaker at anti-Communist rallies and Stephen Myers would invite David whenever there was to be a meeting in his area. Once or twice, David was invited to Ramsey's castle near Arbroath but he himself did not go out of his way to seek the company of either. Stephen Myers still travelled widely throughout Europe and was an excellent conversationalist. As the years went by, he increasingly would contact David whenever he was visiting Glasgow and they would have a leisurely dinner in some quiet restaurant. The two were never what might be called close friends but they had sufficient in common for David to enjoy these occasional evenings.

On one such evening, Myers suggested David might like to visit Germany.

"Why not come with me to Berlin? You'll enjoy it and seeing how Germany's being transformed will be an eye-opener, I promise you."

"Well, I certainly learnt a tremendous amount from my American tour," said David. "Yes, I'd be quite keen to go."

"Great! You'll not regret it. Germany is a positive tonic! Whilst the rest of Europe is still very much in the doldrums the news coming out of Germany is thrilling. Since that fellow Hitler has risen to power, like Mussolini in Italy, he has worked an economic miracle for the Germans. You just wouldn't recognise them as the disheartened nation that had been humiliated at Versailles. Germany is emerging as a confident, thrusting industrial power."

"Certainly, I've read of the efficiency of its industries and of the new spirit of unity among its people. They seem to imposed an acceptable kind of discipline on the youth. That's something this country could do with!"

"Aye! That and a leader determined above all, to resist communism."

So it was agreed that, early in the year 1935, the two would journey to Berlin.

Chapter 13

Perhaps it is true that two people only really get to know one another when they are in each other's company twenty-four hours a day. Certainly in the two days that the voyage from Leith to Bremerhaven lasted, Stephen Myers and David Campbell ceased to be merely social acquaintances and started to become real friends. Their conversation revealed how similar their views were on many subjects, but it was on the development of communism and its potential for destroying their familiar way of life that they really saw eye to eye.

"It's not that I am against the working classes prospering," explained David. "Far from it. However, if the control of the means of production passes into their hands, the result will be chaos. Imagine what would have happened last century as the industrial revolution was getting under way. As wealth was generated, instead of steadily re-investing in factories and machines, workers' committees would have voted to distribute whatever capital was available as increased wages. With no new investment, everything would have stagnated. Instead, the wealth remained in the hands of the mill-owners and was put back into the industry thus raising production, reducing costs and creating work."

"Exactly," replied Stephen. "If the higher wages had been paid, the money would neither have been saved nor spent wisely. All that would have happened is that there would have been even more drunkenness. Certainly any extra would not have been spent on better housing for instance. You mark my words, communism will bankrupt Russia. France looks as if it may go the same way. In fact, if it does not, it will be entirely due to a revitalised Germany standing between it and the Bolsheviks. Thank goodness for Mussolini in Italy and Hitler in Germany."

"Both of them seem to be pulling their people together. Whether it would work in Britain, I don't know," said David. "Our people have been brought up to worship democracy, but they don't seem to notice that it doesn't really work. We're on our sixth prime minister in twelve years. How can you get any continuity or long-term planning when the government changes so often?"

"Very true," added Stephen, "and with an opposition constantly sniping at the government of the day, it's so difficult to carry out essential but unpopular measures. This is where Italy scores. The same is true in Germany. Since Hindenburg died last year, Hitler's power has given him the authority he needs. He is only getting started but already he's made sweeping changes. He's already breaking the Jews' stranglehold on finance and banking. He's rounding up communists and other economic saboteurs. He's forcing gypsies and other vagrants into work-camps. That's the kind of strong government Britain needs. Someone in charge with real authority and power."

"That's the kind of thing Sir Oswald Mosley's been advocating. He's got some kind of a following but you can't say he's uniting the British people," remarked David.

"Mosley's the wrong man!" Stephen continued. "Just you wait until you see Hitler's command over the ordinary German people. They literally worship him! Mosley couldn't hold the candle to Hitler. The way he's stirring things up in London is doing the left-wing parties far more good than harm. Hitler's different. He understands the way the German mind works and he knows how to communicate with his people."

"I can't see the British nation following an Italian or a German model," said David thoughtfully. "Perhaps after some years, when they see the way things develop under Mussolini and Hitler they'll think again, but not now."

"I'm sure you're right, "Stephen replied. "However, in the short term, what Europe needs, indeed, what Britain needs, is a strong Germany manning the eastern frontiers of Europe to keep Stalin from even being tempted."

"Do you really think Stalin would invade western Europe?" David asked.

"Indeed I do!" came the reply. "The only thing that stops him is the fear of a military defeat. That's why a strong Germany is so important. The Poles and the Czechs are neither strong enough nor determined enough to resist. The Austrians and the Swiss are no better. In the long term, I think a united East European Alliance involving all these countries will be the best defence for the whole continent of Europe and that will only come about if Germany gives a very strong lead. Meanwhile, that's why Germany must build up its military strength. Power is the only thing Stalin respects and understands. Hitler cannot stand up to Russia with his hands tied behind his back. France and Britain know that. You mark my words, when Germany enlarges her army and develops an air-force, the politicians of these countries will bluster and protest, but they won't lift a finger to stop Hitler."

"But surely fear of another 1914 situation will make France and Britain resist any attempt by Germany to build up its armed forces," exclaimed David.

"Just wait and see! This year is going to witness tremendous changes in Europe. Germany will finally reject the disarmament clauses of the Versailles Treaty. To save their own faces, the British and French governments will protest to the League of Nations, but nothing will actually be done. So much has changed since 1919! Everyone with any political sense can see that Russia is the new enemy. Germany must be brought on side to help defend the whole of Western Europe. The leaders cannot come out with that kind of fact too publicly. Memories of the War are still too green. Besides, all European nations have their communists and other left-wingers. Any government that spoke out too openly against Stalin and the Reds would find massive opposition. Yet, secretly, they know that Hitler is right. They know he must re-arm Germany. When the final show-down between Russia and the rest of Europe comes, they'll all be grateful for a strong Germany!"

Chapter 14

When the ship eventually berthed at Bremerhaven, Stephen and David went by train to Hamburg. There they were met at their hotel by a German friend of Stephen's, Hans Kandzior. Kandzior, it transpired, was the managing director of a substantial engineering company in the city. After a relaxing evening, it was arranged that the three should tour Kandzior's factory the following day. David found the visit immensely interesting. The Germans were heavily mechanised, although, as he had himself invested in the latest plant at Jayemcee Brassfoundry, David did not feel his own Company lagged too far behind. However, he knew that many other Clydeside firms did. The more disturbing thing, however was the spirit of purpose and unity that was evident in the whole organisation. Although David prided himself in having a dedicated well-motivated staff, there was a discipline and a team spirit among the Germans that he had never seen in Scotland.

Kandzior was clearly an enthusiast for the new National Socialist government.

"Since the War," he explained, "Germany had been floundering. The currency collapsed and the country was hopelessly bankrupt. What was needed was strong leadership. Someone and something to re-unite the people and to give them something to strive for. Hitler has done that! He has set up a real People's government with People's Courts to ensure justice. He's created a new disciplined organisation to bring out the best in the nation's children. He's confiscated the ill-gotten gains that the Jewish financiers and bankers made out of the German people during the War. The working people are happier than they've ever been. There is a new Labour Leisure organisation, 'Strength Through Joy', to help them make the most of their recreational time and holidays. There is going to be a People's car, designed for the German working families, to be sold at a price that will let every German own one."

"Very impressive," said David. "But Herr Hitler does seem to be in confrontation with the League of Nations, especially about re-arming. Surely that is not necessary?"

"On the contrary, it is essential! In the modern world, a country like Germany has to be seen to be strong. It is only by having a really strong army, navy and airforce that Herr Hitler can be sure of not having to use force! It's a paradox, isn't it? Herr Hitler is a man of peace. He doesn't want conflict. But you can only enforce peace if you are strongly armed!"

It did seem a rather contradictory situation. On the one hand, it was true that Germany had to the east an uncomfortably near neighbour in Russia and it was easy to sympathise with the German people's fears of an expanding communist empire. On the other hand, there was something disconcerting about life in this bustling German city. There was an impressive air of efficiency, of unity of purpose, of dedication to building a better future. But there was also a harshness, perhaps high-lighted by the anti-Semitic slogans daubed on business premises owned by Jews, and also by the presence of so many men, women and children in one kind of uniform or another. David had the impression that there might be a bright future in Germany for those who conformed to the new regime's ideals and values, but a difficult time ahead for any dissenters.

In the days that followed, this opinion seemed to be confirmed. He was shown examples of the massive road-building programme and had described to him the complex network of main roads being built to connect all the major centres of the Reich. He visited ship-yards and was greatly impressed by the technology and efficiency of the work force from the management down to the shop-floor. He was shown the 'Strength Through Joy' leisure programme for the workers. It spoke to him of strength, but he was not so sure about the 'joy' part of it. Everything was done with a ruthless, competitive dedication that left very little room for enjoyment. However, he had to admit that it suited the German personality and seemed to work there, whilst he was sure it would not work on Clydeside. In due time, the trip came to an end and Stephen and David took ship for Leith.

"I do hope that Hitler is not going to provoke another war," said David. "But if there ever were another, I would much rather have the Germans on my side than against me! There is something awe-inspiring about their dedication. You get the impression that once started they would be unstoppable!"

"Don't worry!" replied Stephen. "There's not going to be a war. One day there may have to be a battle to stop once and for all Stalin's ambition but when that happens German, French, Italian and British soldiers will fight shoulder to shoulder against the Bolsheviks."

"Should we be backing Mosley and the British Fascists then?" asked David.

"No, I don't think so. The big difference between Hitler and Mosley is that Hitler has the support of the overwhelming majority of the German people. He understands them and they have united under him. Mosley is better at dividing people. He really has very little support and that comes from fanatics. No! I think you and I can perhaps serve the interests of Britain best by continuing to observe from the side-lines without being too obviously influenced by either Hitler or Mosley. One day, we may be required to take action to hamper the ambitions of Stalin and his allies in the British Communist Party and we may be best able to do this if we seem to have no political affiliation."

David was more than happy to fall in with this assessment, partly because it did make good sense, but perhaps more because it suited his temperament to avoid having to take a very public stand about anything.

Chapter 15

Once back in Scotland, David concentrated once more on his business life. The worst of the slump was past and Clydeside was becoming increasingly busy. The ship-building yards again rang with the sound of cranes, of steam-engines, of the clang of metal on metal, all accompanied by the machine-gun-like rattle of the rivitors turning sheets of steel into sea-going vessels. The renewed prosperity did not, however, diminish the under-lying discontent among the work-force. The communist agitators continued their corrosive work, stimulating strife.

The news from abroad was very mixed. There was much to encourage David. Mussolini had secured his position in Rome by nationalising the Italian Banks. By the middle of 1936, his popularity was at an all-time high when he brought the conflict in Ethiopia to a successful close, establishing an Italian Empire in Africa. Myer's predictions about Hitler largely proved justified. The announcement of a German Airforce being established came and went, hardly causing a ripple. Germany reoccupied the Rhineland, territory that had been taken from them by the Treaty of Versailles. There were loud protests about this, but no action. In the east, the German minorities in Austria, Hungary and

Czechoslovakia were claiming that they were being oppressed and Hitler warned repeatedly that if the respective governments did not act, he would. In the spring of 1938, Germany annexed Austria and, later that year, the Sudetenland became part of Germany as a result of the Munich settlement. Whilst these events caused great misgivings in the country as a whole, David was neither surprised nor worried by them. He understood that Germany had to enlarge its territories and build up its forces if the Russian menace was to be contained. The farther east the frontiers of the German-controlled territories were, the better for the whole of Europe.

If anyone had any doubts about the communist threat, they only had to look at Spain, where all-out civil war was raging between General Franco and the communists. The communists were receiving aid from the Russians and also from left-wingers in almost every European country. There were an estimated 35,000 fighting on the communist side who were not Spanish. These formed an International Brigade and among them were some 5,000 from Britain and the United States. David worried lest the infection spread to the rest of Europe and civil wars became rife. It was relief, then, that he watched the air-forces of Italy and Germany come in strongly and decisively on General Franco's side and the Communist forces compelled to capitulate.

At one of their infrequent evenings in a Glasgow restaurant in the late spring of 1939, Stephen and David talked over the current events in Europe.

"Hitler has gone a long way towards securing the

eastern frontiers of Europe against the Bolsheviks," said Myers. "However, there remains the problem of Poland. The Polish army is incredibly obsolete. They still pride themselves in their cavalry, as if men and horses, however brave, can do anything if Russian tanks start to roll. Stalin is biding his time, but he will strike west when he is ready. He is probably worried lest Germany eventually becomes too strong, so the chances are he'll attack sooner rather than later. The trouble is, he'll steam-roller across Poland and Germany will have to stop him far too far west. Poland refuses to co-operate with Hitler and seems to want to provoke conflict with him."

"If war breaks out between Germany and Poland, won't Britain and France support Poland?" asked David.

"They'll protest, as usual," came the reply, "but they won't fight. The rest of Europe knows that Germany is the lynch-pin in any international strategy to contain the communists. No! What's more likely to happen is that war will break out between Poland and Germany. Poland will provoke it, even though it may be Germany who ultimately fires the first shot. The Russians will then attack Poland from the east and France and Britain will have to come in on Germany's side. It's a pity if it does have to come to a scrap, but it will be worth it in the end if Russia gets trounced once and for all by the combined might of the western European states."

Chapter 6

Stephen Myer's predictions had been so uncannily accurate in all the time he had known him, that David was not greatly surprised to learn from the BBC news that war had broken out between Germany and Poland. Nor was he surprised when France and Britain entered their protests at Germany's actions. They had protested so many times before that he was sure it would come to nothing. It therefore came as a terrible shock to learn that Britain had declared war on Germany. David listened in horror to the sombre voice of the Prime Minister on the radio that Sunday morning, the 3rd of September 1939. He switched the wireless off and sat with his head in his hands.

"How can they be so stupid?" he muttered again and again. "Germany's not our enemy! We're declaring war on the wrong country! There'll be needless bloodshed and, whatever the outcome, Europe'll still have to fight the Russians!"

He had his own position to consider. What should his policy be? Should he throw the weight of Jayemcee Brassfoundry manufacturing capacity in with the Government? Switch to manufacturing the tools for war-fare? Should he campaign as a pacifist? This idea he dismissed immediately. He was not a pacifist. If war had been declared against Stalin, he would have been whole-heartedly behind it. But against Hitler? If he refused to use his business in the production of war materials, the Government would simply commandeer it. He would find himself an outcast and no doubt would receive no compensation.

David forced himself to come to some sort of decision. The confiscation of his business assets by the British Government was no more palatable than confiscation by communists. Becoming a pariah would help no-one. Without wealth or prestige, he could not hope to bring about change. And change, he felt, must come. The insanity of the capitalist countries of Europe tearing themselves apart whilst the Russian jackal sat on the side-lines waiting to pounce on the weak and the injured was so evident that sooner or later sound sense must prevail. It went against the grain, but he decided that he must appear to support to the hilt the Chamberlain Government. Later in the day he made contact by telephone with Stephen Myers and the two arranged to meet.

Myers was as taken aback by the turn of events as was David. Over the past five years, Hitler had repeatedly defied the League of Nations which, in turn, had proved itself a toothless tiger. Why Britain and France had changed so radically now was beyond him. Myers, however, had contacts all over Europe and he had arranged to meet with one or two in the neutral Republic of Ireland. Travel to Northern Ireland was still easy enough in those September days and the border to the Irish Republic open. David agreed to meet with Myers and his friends. It seemed unwise to travel together so they left Stranraer on different ferries and did not meet up again until they had reached the sleepy Irish village of Clane, a few miles outside Dublin. David was ostensibly visiting Dublin because he was negotiating the purchase of specialised calibrating machinery. He did indeed buy the equipment, but no doubt would have delegated the trip to someone else but for the desire to go to Clane.

Chapter 17

At a secluded old mansion on the outskirts of Clane, David was introduced to James O'Neill and Reinhard Bielfeld. O'Neill was a middle-aged Irishman who, it was explained to David, was the proprietor of a medium-size business specialising in the manufacture of short-wave radios. His products were marketed through agents in several cities throughout Europe and he himself was widely travelled. Bielfeld was Swiss and was concerned with finance. David was not told anything very specific, but was left with the impression that Bielfeld looked after the investment funds of people of various nationalities, including both German and British. It soon became clear that all four, though from such different backgrounds, shared a deep fear of Russia and of international communism.

"Britain and France should never have declared war," stated Bielfeld emphatically. "Surely they can see that the farther east the frontiers of capitalist Europe and communist Russia the better! You have only to see how quickly Stalin marched into eastern Poland to realise that sooner or later he had intended to take over the whole country. I've no doubt that Hitler's intelligence service was warning him of an impending Russian attack on Poland and that's why he got his blow in first. If he had not attacked, the Russian army would have taken over all of Poland, not just the east."

"And how do you see things developing from here?" David asked.

"I think that the Russians and the Germans will establish a frontier and settle down in defensive positions. If France and Britain had not declared war, Hitler would have gone on the offensive and pushed the Reds right back. Now, he will want to wait and see how things develop in the west. The Germans will not want to fight on two fronts. If the Allies do not attack, he will probably take on Russia. Then all the French and British governments should do is to let Hitler sort out the communist problem once and for all. Once Hitler has won in the east, they can negotiate an armistice. The worst thing that can happen is for all out war to break out between the Allies and Germany. All that will produce is a much weakened Germany. Stalin will wait and, when he judges that the combatants are all near exhaustion, he will attack Germany. If the Germans are forced westwards into France and the Netherlands, the Russian army will follow. You mark my words, they won't stop until they reach the Atlantic. Even then they won't stop. They'll swarm across the Channel and Britain and Eire will fall to them."

"So the only hope for Europe is a German victory?" asked Stephen.

"No, I didn't say that. A German defeat will be a disaster for Europe, but Hitler does not need to defeat Britain and France. An honourable draw would be the ideal, with territorial gains for Germany in the east."

"So what should our policy be, do you suggest?" James O'Neill asked, coming into the conversation for the first time. "My country is, of course, neutral and some fools are silly enough to think that Hitler or Stalin, whichever gets here first, will simply take over Ulster and respect our neutrality. Talk about living in cloud-cookoo land! From my point of view, there's not much I can do at present. Perhaps as things develop it may become clearer but meanwhile I think all I can do is to sit and watch."

"That's probably true for all of us," said Bielfeld. "We can do little at present, but we should think things through so that we know what we'll do if Russia does enter the war. As time goes on, we may not be able to meet like this, so it would be wise to have a co-ordinated strategy in mind now."

"We may not be able to meet," said O'Neill, "but we can still stay in touch. I can provide each of you with the very latest in short-wave radios and we can contact each other even if other means of communication break down."

"Radio's all very well," remarked Stephen, "but you never know who else may be listening!"

"True, but we can devise a code that will stop either side being able to eavesdrop. A simple book code is very hard to break. All we need do is to agree on a particular book which we all have access to and decide in advance a sequence of pages taken at random from it. The first message might, for instance, be taken from page four. The message can then be put together as a sequence of pairs of numbers. The first number is the line on the page. The second is the word in that line. As two numbers express a word of any length, it should be possible to pass even quite a long message very quickly, which might be a very important factor if the Russians are trying to locate the transmitter. As you would never need to use the same page twice, cracking such a code is nearly impossible."

"All right, so we stay in touch," said David "but what then? We can keep each other informed of the situation as each of us sees it from his perspective. Yes, I can see that would be helpful, but what if Russia does attack, how can we help stop them?"

"That we must assess at the time," said Bielfeld. "It may mean we have to take some very hard decisions and be very far-sighted. For instance, if things are going badly for Germany in the east and the Russians are advancing, we may be able to influence public opinion in favour of a cease-fire in the west that will let the Germans concentrate on Stalin. We'll just have to wait and see. The important thing will be to have made some preparations now to keep as many options as possible open for the future."

So it was agreed. Much of the remaining time was taken up with learning how to get the best out of short-wave radios and in setting up their own private code. The decision was taken to base this on the Encyclopaedia Britannica. There was nothing remotely suspicious about men of their status having this in their book-shelves and the scope for variety of volumes and pages was nearly unlimited. The only fore-seeable problem would be if any of them were forced to operate away from home. It was agreed that if that happened, they would move on to using the New Testament. This was definitely only to be an emergency measure, however. It had the disadvantage of lacking modern technical terms. It was also a book that a skilled code-cracker might guess was the basis. Its big advantage was that it was so readily available that the sender need not necessarily carry his own personal copy with him. Any parish church would be bound to be able to supply one.

David agreed that his newly acquired calibrating machinery would be shipped from Dublin to Scotland by a particular machinery packing and removal company recommended by O'Neill. Although it was not spelt out to him, he realised that this was how the short-wave radios for Stephen Myers and himself were to enter Scotland.

Chapter 18

The months that followed were a time of confusing emotions for David. To begin with, it looked like stalemate on the Continent. The French had taken up defensive positions. The British had despatched an Expeditionary Army to northern France, but no one was doing much fighting. Even the much feared air-raids did not come, or at least, not with horrific consequences that had been predicted. In England, in particular, it was fashionable to talk about "the phoney war". At sea, there was more action and the German submarines were soon scoring notable successes. However, in the east there was no movement. The frontier between Russian and German forces had been established and there was no fighting at all there.

Then in the spring of 1940, it all changed. The German forces attacked France through Belgium, thus walking round the elaborate French defences. In a matter of weeks the French army was battered into submission. The British retreated to Dunkirk and were successfully evacuated by the Navy. Hitler over-ran Belgium, Holland and Denmark. He already held Norway and so, by the summer of 1940, he was master of Europe. David's feelings were ambivalent. On the one hand, he could not help being relieved to see this strong all-conquering army between Britain and Russia. On the other hand, he realised that Hitler was unlikely to stop at the Channel. It was only a matter of time before the British Isles were invaded and David, for all that he wanted an undefeated Germany, certainly did not want Britain to follow France and be occupied by Germans.

The summer of that year was marked by growing anxiety about the impending invasion. It was also marked by increased bombing of targets in the west of Scotland as more German airforce planes attacked the Glasgow area. The vast docks and ship-building yards were an obvious target. The crucially important Rolls-Royce factories were another. However, there was little excitement at Dumbarton at this early stage of the war and virtually none at all at Helensburgh and Blairgowrie.

James O'Neill had provided two radio sets for David. One he concealed in the cellar of his house at Helensburgh. The other he took to Blairgowrie. The need for either seemed to have receded as the communists did not look like being players in the war at all. However, he moved the Blairgowrie set, first to his cottage up the glen, and then to the secret cave. It was during this period that he installed a simple low-voltage lighting system at the glen cottage. Its power source was a wind-powered generator which David devised from a car dynamo. The electricity was stored in large accumulators, but he also kept two large car batteries fully charged. They would not be very easy to transport, but, if he needed to, he could carry them to the cave to power the radio.

As summer gave way to autumn, the war in the air

hotted up, although the main impact of this was far away to the south. Whilst David knew there was much aerial combat going on, like most of his fellow countrymen, he only realised that the all-important Battle of Britain was being lost and won when it was over. Not that peace followed. The bombing raids increased, although it was London that bore the brunt at this stage. Clydeside, however was not unscathed, and regularly throughout the late autumn and early winter a dozen or more bombers would scream across the skies and drop their bombs with varying levels of accuracy and effectiveness. All this was only a prelude to what was to come.

On the evening of Thursday 13th March 1941, David was still at work in Dumbarton when the air-raid sirens went. Shortly after 9 o'clock, the sky started to throb with the sound of aircraft engines. Soon it was clear that this was no ordinary raid and David decided that discretion was the better part of valour. He hurried to an air-raid shelter. It was already crammed with many of his own staff as well as others. The noise was deafening as 250 Luftwaffe raiders poured out their deadly loads on Clydeside. The worst destruction was farther up river at Clydebank where the bombers inflicted terrible damage. The raid went on hour after hour and by dawn it seemed as if the whole of the town of Clydebank was destroyed or was on fire. Dumbarton was hit repeatedly, but got off comparatively lightly. Although the casualty figures were not made public at the time, everyone on Clydeside knew the toll was horrific. The fires burned on out of control. Broken water mains meant that there was no water pressure available to the fire-fighters. Fire-engines ran out of petrol and stopped pumping. It was into the following week before the situation was brought under control. The dead were buried in mass graves. The smouldering fires were finally extinguished. Work recommenced in the docks and shipyards.

For David, this was a turning point. Prior to the Clydebank raid, he had no particular hatred of the Germans. Now, he saw them as a force for evil that must be stopped. He had shared in the hardships of the days and nights following the raid. He had worked hard and heroically alongside his staff as they dug the survivors out of the ruined houses. He had endured the dangers of fire-fighting, even when sporadic lone raiders were still using the fire to guide their bombing raids. His standing in the eyes of his staff and of the community was enhanced as never before, although the desire for popularity or the esteem of others in no way motivated him.

The foundry was damaged. Several buildings were beyond repair. The main yard was pitted with bomb-craters. However, two days with bull-dozers and lorries and the debris was gone. The yard was flat once more and work had already started rebuilding what was essential, whilst several smaller buildings were destined never to be replaced.

Chapter 19

The March air-raids had really brought the war to David's back-yard. Now at first hand, he had seen the destructive power of the Luftwaffe. Dumbarton had taken a battering and it was with some relief that David would return to snatch some sleep at Helensburgh. However, there were changes there as well.

David knew that various buildings had been requisitioned by the War office for military purposes such as billets for naval personnel while their ships were undergoing repairs, dispersed office accommodation for the Admiralty staff and so on. It therefore came as no surprise when he was told his house was required as rest and recuperation quarters for Royal Navy officers between voyages. He did manage to negotiate for his being permitted to occupy a small servants' flat at the top of the house. Into its two small rooms, he packed everything of sentimental value and still managed to leave just enough space in which to sleep. The only area for sitting was in a turret window. There David set up a pair of battle-ship binoculars which had once been mounted on one of the German fleet that had been scuttled at Scapa Flow in 1919. From this lofty vantage-point, David commanded a view of the shipping in the upper Clyde.

The arrangement was not without its advantages. He could mix freely with the Navy types who lived downstairs and snack in their officers' mess. That he was left with only enough room to sleep did not trouble him. His life these days consisted of little else but work and sleep. When he did take time off, it was much better that this be in Perthshire anyway.

It was purely coincidental that David was working at Blairgowrie at the beginning of May. Seldom a night had gone by since the night of the big Clydebank air-raid without the sound of air-raid sirens. The throb of bombers filled the skies above the River Clyde. There was the constant chatter of machine guns, the heavier crump of anti-aircraft fire and

the thunderous roar of high explosive bombs and falling masonry. However, the raiders came in small numbers. Sometimes one lone bomber was all that was seen in a whole night. The result was a continuing interruption of production in the docks and shipyards, to say nothing of the strain on the nerves of the entire community. On the 6th of May, the Luftwaffe returned in force. During the night, over 180 bombers struck at the Clyde. Using Loch Lomond as a marker, they flew in from the east, swung south down the Gareloch and banked round to face eastwards again, pouring out their deadly cargoes on the docks, the warehouses, the shipyards and the homes that lined both banks of the river. The factory at Dumbarton suffered a direct hit and several of David's staff died instantly. Had it not been for his absence at Blairgowrie, there is little doubt that David himself would have died with them.

The fires were still burning when, the following night, another slightly smaller bomber force struck. Guided by the blazing buildings and oil-storage tanks, they pressed home their attack. The damage to property was again devastating, although the loss of life considerably less. The BBC broadcast a very limited description of the raid and its effects. Despite this watered down version of events, David realised that there was again serious trouble in the west. The telephone lines were down, of course, so he was unable to contact the Dumbarton factory to get a first-hand account. Fearing the worst, he took the first train he could. The journey took hours, with repeated hold-ups that became more frequent as the train drew near Glasgow. At several points, the bombs had blasted the lines or the bridges or the signalling system. However, at last he reached the factory and started to take over the management of the repair work. The loss of equipment was less serious than he might have feared. The loss of key personnel was much more alarming. The factory had been concentrating on casting and milling the thousands of brass components essential to the ships that the Clydeside yards were working on round the clock. Everything from port-hole frames to the mounts for guns and the fittings for life-boats had been being mass-produced. Mercifully, the stores of patterns and moulds had escaped the destructive power of the bombs. Several lathes were beyond repair and production would be greatly reduced. Scarcely pausing for food or sleep, David threw himself into the task of replacing the ruined plant as best he could and of recruiting and training replacement staff.

In the midst of all this activity there occurred one of the strangest incidents of the war. During the night of the 10th of May, a lone German fighter circled the skies over moorland south of Glasgow. The pilot bailed out and parachuted safely to earth. The plane crashed. The German was taken into custody. He demanded to be taken to the Duke of Hamilton, a demand that was naturally enough ignored. However, it emerged in interrogation that the prisoner was no ordinary pilot. He was, in fact, Rudolph Hess, Hitler's deputy. His increasingly angry demands to be taken to someone in government were ignored. He was imprisoned for the duration of the war and, eventually, brought to trial with the other leading Nazis accused of war crimes and crimes against humanity. Bits and pieces of this bizarre event filtered out to the press and David was also able to pick up unpublished detail from rather indiscreet army officer friends. The whole incident was puzzling, but as it seemed to be just an irrelevant side-show, David did not dwell on it.

Chapter 20

On one of his rare evenings off, David met up with Stephen Myers.

"The Hun has been hitting us in a big way," he said. "Do you think this is all a prelude to invasion?"

"No, I don't think so. The right time for an invasion was last autumn, but the RAF gave the Luftwaffe so much to think about that they called it off. Now it would take much greater forces than it would have then. I think Hitler doesn't dare concentrate all his strength on the assault on Britain because he fears Stalin will stab him in the back."

"Do you really think so?" David asked. "I thought that, after the two of them had finished carving up Poland, they were getting on quite well together. They do have a non-aggression treaty, after all."

"Aye, but a treaty either of them would break if they felt it were to their advantage. Some of my friends reckon that Stalin is poised to hit Germany this summer."

"Well, that will certainly take some of the heat off us if he does! Having to fight on two fronts will give the Germans immense problems. Would it not be best if the two of them slogged it out for a year or two and, when both were practically exhausted, the British could invade?"

81

"That sounds good in theory, but what if Stalin were to get the upper hand? If he pushed the Germans back, the British would have to come in on Hitler's side or, eventually, to face the victorious Russians who won't want to stop once they feel they are on a winning streak."

"Wouldn't the Americans come in before it reached that point. Surely they wouldn't sit back and let the whole of Europe fall to the communists, would they?"

Myers replied gloomily, "They seem quite prepared to let Hitler take over Europe without intervening. I think it would be the same if it were Stalin. There's such a strong non-interventionist lobby in the States. They're determined not to get drawn into any European war. In some ways, you can hardly blame them. With the whole of the Atlantic between them and us, they can afford to stand on the side-lines and spectate. No doubt their businessmen will look forward to resuming normal trade relations with whoever wins. It's not their war, not their problem. Why should they shed American blood in distant lands? Only the most far-sighted could be expected to see that, if they don't come to the conflict, then one day the conflict will come to them."

"It's really very short-sighted of them," commented David. "Whether it's the Nazis or the Russians who end up dominating all of Europe plus a major part of Asia, one day America will have to stand up to them The evidence of history is that conquerors want to go on conquering. They don't just stop. They have to be stopped. I've often thought that had I been a Roman at the height of the Roman conquests, I would have been content with all the beautiful lands of Italy, France, Germany, Spain and England. I would have taken a quick look at Scotland's wilderness of mountains and bogs and decided enough was enough. One winter of sleet, frost and snow plus one summer of rain and midges would have convinced me. But Hadrian and Company? No! They had to slog it out for two or three centuries before they learnt!"

"The communists have an avowed policy of spreading their doctrines throughout the world. In practice, that means that they are committed to war and to conquest. Hitler, on the other hand seems to be obsessed with the idea of world domination by his 'master race'. The two are on a collision course. I should say that it's only a matter of time before one or other acts. My bet is that Russia will strike first. So long as Churchill is Prime-Minister, I can't see us making common cause with Hitler. If we don't, however, I think we may live to regret it."

David was frankly appalled at the very idea of becoming allies of the Nazis, however much he feared and hated the communists.

"If you'd been with me in Clydebank, "he said, "nothing would make you willing to be an ally of Hitler! The suffering and destruction was beyond description."

"I do sympathise and I am not for one moment in favour of a German victory. However, we may be forced to decide which is the lesser of two evils. Hitler and his thugs are evil beyond doubt, but there are decent Germans too. If the war were going badly for Hitler, I think they would overthrow him and sue for peace with us before the Russians overwhelmed them. You remember that business of Hess? I wonder if he wasn't on some kind of peace mission."

"If he was, Hitler certainly doesn't seem to have been behind it," replied David. "The Germans have more or less disowned Hess as suffering from over-work and suggested that he's had some kind of break-down."

"But supposing he knew that Hitler was about to invade Russia? Or suppose German intelligence had wind of an imminent Russian invasion? Is it possible that Hess was sent to try to secure an armistice in the west so that the Germans would not have to fight on two fronts?"

"I can't see Hitler offering any kind of peace deal at this stage," was David's comment. "Things are going really well for him. He doesn't have to fight on two fronts. It will be a year or more before Britain could possibly land an army on the Continent. If Hess were on a peace mission, it wasn't the Nazis who sent him. He was either acting alone or some underground movement in Germany sent him. Time will tell, though. If fighting does break out between Germany and Russia, it won't prove anything about Hess, but it may be a pointer as to what he was up to."

"Either way," said Myres, "I don't think any of this will affect us in the short term." With that, the conversation drifted off on to other more trivial matters.

Chapter 21

On the 22nd of June, David and the rest of the world learned with some amazement that the German Army had invaded Soviet Russia. News was naturally sketchy at first, but as the days went by, it became clear that, by any standard, the Nazi forces were sweeping all before them. The Russian Air Force was more or less put out of action completely. More of its planes were destroyed on the ground than were shot down in combat. The Blitzkrieg advance of the Germans seemed unstoppable. Day after day, their armies pressed on eastwards on an 1800 mile front. The ill-equipped, ill-trained and ill-led Communist army retreated everywhere. The advance was halted eventually, not by military success by the Russians, but by the onset of winter. The German successes had exceeded their own most optimistic forecasts and their supply lines were dangerously extended and vulnerable. As the grim Russian winter set in, the average German soldier began to discover that his clothing and his military equipment were most inadequate for what lay ahead.

The British Prime Minister, Winston Churchill, announced at a very early stage that all possible help would be given to the Russians. For long enough, any such support was more psychological than real. Russia was steadily losing the territories in which its manufacturing capability was based. Although whole foundries and factories were moved eastwards before the Germans could reach them, Russian munitions production was decimated. If the Soviet Union was going to be kept in the war, Britain would have to supply arms and ammunition. However, the carrying out of such a strategy could not be set up overnight and it would clearly be some months before a significant contribution to Stalin's needs could be made.

In the Autumn, James O'Neill visited Scotland and he and Stephen Myers arranged to meet David in Blairgowrie.

"Seems you were right about war between Hitler and Stalin," said David as he greeted Myers. "I thought you might be at the time, but I never imagined it would be so soon."

"I imagine that Hitler decided that the Soviets would strike later on in the Autumn and that he had better strike the first blow and catch them on the hop."

"He certainly did that," exclaimed O'Neill. "He's pushing them steadily back and all the time cutting them off from some of their most important sources of supply. Russia is an enormous place and Stalin can keep retreating until the German supply lines are so ridiculously long that Hitler will have to call a halt. Eventually, there will be a stalemate. Hitler will not want the front line to be two or three thousand miles from Germany. Russia will be so short of all kinds of supplies that they won't be able to push them back. Then both will have to dig in and form defensive positions."

"That can only help us, can't it?" asked David. "After all, if Hitler is tied up in the east, he can't invade here."

"True," said O'Neill, "but he's supporting the Italians in North Africa. If they defeat our forces there we'll lose Egypt, the Suez Canal and our supply lines to the east. Furthermore, it will open the way for Hitler to get oil from the Persian Gulf. There's an awful lot to play for in that sector of the war and Hitler knows it!"

"At any rate, the fear of a Russian advance seems to have been very nicely taken care of," replied David. "If Stalin and Hitler fight it out on battlefields six or seven hundred miles into Russia, we can only benefit. I am a bit worried about Churchill supplying the Russians with arms, though. I know we want to keep them in the war, but, if we misjudge the situation and give too much help, Germany might suddenly collapse and we'll find the Red Army at Calais!"

"Well, that's one of the things we wanted to speak to you about," said Stephen Myers. "There's no serious threat at present, but we feel we ought to monitor the situation and make sure we know what is going on. Everybody knows that Britain is giving aid to the Russians. Only those in government really know how much. We think we ought to gather as much intelligence as we can so that we have some sort of feel as to what is going on."

"Getting information is one thing," replied David. "Knowing what to do with it is another. I agree that we would like to know just how much aid is reaching Stalin. What on earth do we do if we reach the conclusion that it is excessive?"

"That might call for some hard decisions. However, the important thing at present is to get our finger on the pulse so that we know as accurately as possible what is going on." said O'Neill.

"And how do you think I can help?" asked David. "My own position here in Blairgowrie is almost totally insulated from the war. Dumbarton is different, but I still have only a very limited idea of what's going on."

"Yes, naturally we understand that," replied O'Neill. "None of us has anything like a true picture of what's happening. That's what makes it all a bit frightening. Churchill is so single-minded in working for Hitler's downfall that he may not realise how big a problem he's building up until it's much too late. If we can get enough sources of information pooling their findings, we should be able to give the country early warning and, if necessary, work for a change of Prime Minister so that we get the country led by someone with a proper sense of the Red menace. Now, your foundry supplies the ship-builders and ship-repairers, am I right?"

"Yes, everything that is made from copper or brass. That includes military things like gun-mounts, direction-finding instrument parts, periscope parts and so on for the war-ships and all kinds of fittings for the Merchant Navy. How does that help, though?"

O'Neill went on, "You are then in a position to know or to make intelligent guesses as to which ships are bound for the Arctic convoys. If you can relay to us, even in the most general terms the size of each convoy and some idea of when it is sailing this will help. We can then add this to information from other sources and keep an eye on the situation.

Churchill does not have it all his own way in Parliament, you know and there are a number of MPs who share our anxieties. They, too, have difficulty getting the big picture. The government tends only to tell even Parliament the bare minimum. If we build up a dossier on aid to Russia, we can leak it to key back-benchers at the appropriate time. The important thing is that we must be well-informed."

"How do I communicate any information that I may glean?" David asked. "Is this where we start using the short-wave radios?"

"Yes, that would probably be best. Strictly speaking it is against the law, but as we'll be communicating in code, the enemy could not benefit and the authorities, even if they do pick up the transmissions, won't know what they're about."

"Won't they be able to use direction-finding equipment to locate the source of the transmissions?" David asked anxiously. He did not mind helping, but was worried about the legal implications.

"In theory they can. In practice, direction-finding is so slow that, if you are on the air for only fifteen minutes at a time, they haven't a hope. It shouldn't be too difficult to re-site the radio-sets at frequent intervals so they will not be able to anticipate where the next transmission will come from. Don't worry about it. Just keep your messages as short as possible. We can streamline our codes so that a single letter can stand for a certain size or type of ship. Likewise, departure points and destinations can be expressed with one, or at the most, two letters. In that way we should be able to say a tremendous amount in a matter of a minute or two."

"How will we know when to transmit?" Asked Myers.

"Simple! At the end of each message, you sign off with the date and time of the next. As this will be coded, only we will know when that will be."

"And what if, for any reason we cannot transmit at the time we said we would?" David asked. "Something might easily crop up to delay me and I would not just be able to drop everything to get to the radio."

"If you fail to make the transmission, you try again at the same time the next day. If you transmit but receive no acknowledgement, you try again later. If we decide a simple formula, the second transmission can be an odd number of minutes after the first. In that way, if anyone overheard the first, he would be totally unable to guess the probable time of the second. We can further complicate the arrangement, by frequent changes in wave-length."

So the three settled down to working out a simple, easily memorised series of code-words and numbers to add to their Encyclopaedia Britannica code. By the end of the evening, they had a satisfactory system worked out and dates agreed for the first transmissions.

Chapter 22

When David returned to Dumbarton after the week-end, he arrived at the office about noon. There he was met by Jimmy McDuff.

"As if poor Glasgow didn't have enough problems what with the war, it seems there's a sex-fiend on the loose."

"Why? Whatever's happened?"

"Some poor kiddie from the Gorbals. Found dead behind a midden. The official word is that the police are treating it as a suspicious death, but a pal who's a copper told me that poor wretch had been knifed. Practically disembowelled, he said."

"Oh dear me!" exclaimed David. "Running a killer like that to earth is desperately difficult at the best if times. What with the blackout and so many people throughout the country being on the move one way or another, finding the murderer will be next to impossible. Have the police any ideas?"

"Nothing to go on, as I understand it. The last murder of this kind was about five years ago. They strung the man up in Barlinnie so whoever else did this one, it wasn't him. That's one thing in favour of hanging: the murderer doesn't repeat his crime!"

"I'd certainly have no mercy on anyone who killed a kiddie. But they've got to find him first. You know, if they don't catch someone like that more or less in the act, it must be terribly difficult to find him. I wonder what a child-killer looks like?"

"Very ordinary, I imagine. There are probably no give-away signs. I only hope the coppers get him quickly, or there'll be more killings to come, you mark my words."

. . . .

In his cheap tenement lodgings in Glasgow's Maryhill, Arthur Nelson lay back on his bed and replayed in his mind the excitement of the previous Saturday evening. Glasgow would be a happy hunting ground for him. The back streets teemed with unsupervised kids of all ages. Almost all the men-folk were either in the forces or were working all the hours there were in this great industrial city. The not-infrequent bombing raids added to the general confusion. And of course, the blackout was a god-send. No one thought anything of a dark figure walking the streets or taking a short-cut through a bomb-site. He had been three weeks in Glasgow now, was well-established in the big steel-works down the road and had a land-lady who was a part-time bar-maid and therefore predictably out every evening until after closing time. His new identity ensured that his past would not catch up with him. Bromley and his tense days as a fugitive living in a cellar were comfortably part of the distant past now.

There had been a fair bit of blood, but he'd been able to clean up completely long before his land-lady had returned. Indeed, by the time she did come home, he was off to do his stint on night-shift. Luck was on his side in that the boy was not missed from home until nearly 11pm. Then the body was not found until mid-morning and so the police could not be at all sure of the time of death. The probability was that they would assume it was later than it had actually been. With a spot of luck, he would have the excellent alibi of being at work with dozens of others. Yes! Glasgow had a lot going for it!

Chapter 23

That week-end David cycled up to his glen cottage. Petrol rationing had become steadily more severe as the war went on. David, being involved in essential war work, got extra coupons but was generally scrupulous about not misusing these. He had foreseen the shortage and had bought three bicycles and adequate tyres and other spares to see him through many years. Cycling also had the merit of keeping him fit which was important as he no longer could spend as much time as he would have liked on the hills.

This trip was not merely for pleasure. He had brought with him a long length of copper wire. The weather on the Saturday was appalling. The rain lashed down and this, together with a thick mist, cut visibility to a matter of yards. However, this suited his purpose. He slipped out of the cottage soon after dawn and made his way by a round-about route to the cave. Secure in the knowledge that the mist and rain screened him completely, he set about rigging a carefully concealed aerial system. The radio was as he had left it in the cave. Very carefully he placed the set itself deep in the cave and built a cocoon of rocks around it. When he was finished no-one would guess its presence. All he had to do was to remove two judiciously placed rocks to expose the dials, controls and terminals. The aerial was concealed outside and the last twenty feet could readily be unwound and connected to the set. All he needed was the batteries and he could transmit.

When he had completed his work, David very carefully gathered up every last trace of his ever having been there. In the highly unlikely event of anyone ever discovering the radio, there was absolutely nothing that could be traced back to him. By the time he had made a circuitous trek back to the cottage, he was soaked to the skin and chilled to the marrow. He was, however, well pleased with his day's work.

On Sunday evening he returned to Helensburgh. Although he was still, at least in theory, master of the house, in practice only his small flat in the turret was exclusively his. It was, to put it mildly, somewhat over-furnished as he had packed into its small space everything that he considered of sentimental value. The cellar, too was his private store. However, whilst he was able to store the second radio there, he considered it much too risky to transmit from there. After much thought, he decided to take the risk of transferring it to an attic space above the pattern store at Dumbarton. The store was a vital part of the foundry. There the moulds and patterns for any part that might ever be required in future were kept. As it was so important, it was a strongly built and very secure building. Only a few trusted staff had access to it. This meant that the risk of one of the staff stumbling on the radio was low. However, if it were found, because several others had access to the store, the finger of suspicion would not point to David alone.

Some months earlier, when the bombing had brought down some of the telephone wires, David had arranged for part of the system to be re-routed underground. This made it less likely to be damaged either by a bomb-blast or, more mundanely, by a crane crossing the yard. The old lines, now disconnected at both ends, still ran from the end of the building via three telephone poles to the perimeter of the yard where they abruptly terminated. David had already ear-marked this as a potential aerial and, on one of the many nights when he was working on into the small hours on his own, he had connected up a carefully concealed cable that enabled the telephone wires to be linked up to the store attic space. He had also linked up a mains voltage cable to take power to the set, via a transformer. This was all camouflaged and only a detailed study might reveal that it was something not connected to the multitude of other wires and cables that ran through every part of the building.

Now all he needed was something to transmit. The date for his first transmission came and he sent a short coded message which gave his call-sign, said [in code, of course], 'nothing to report', and ended with a time and date for his next signal. It all seemed very simple, but David still got something of a thrill when the code letters for 'received and understood' came through.

The turret room provided a certain amount of information. Through the old German battleship binoculars, he was able to watch a remarkable amount of the shipping on the Clyde. He would spend a little time there around high tide as often as possible. Smaller ships were not so much restricted by the level of the tide, but the larger vessels could only move a couple of hours either side of high tide.

More productive of information were the various service men who used the NAFFI facilities downstairs. There were never any civilians around in the evenings and the naval personnel in particular were remarkably indiscreet. David was accepted as one of them and, although he was careful never to ask a direct question, he became adept at learning what was going on.

At this stage, most of what he was able to pass on was history by the time he learned about it. For instance, in the middle of October he was able to give a sketchy summary of the first of the British convoys round the northern tip of Norway to the Russian port of Archangel. It had sailed from Liverpool in mid-August and returned via the Orkneys in early October. It was only by overhearing the exchange of experiences of various naval officers that he formed some picture of what had happened.

The following weeks brought more news of more convoys. With these came stories of increasing trouble with snow and ice. At this stage in the story of the Arctic convoys, there was practically no serious problems caused by the enemy. The problems were the consequences of the harsh weather and these worsened as the Arctic winter set in. David was drawn increasingly into these conversations as officers described the problems of trying to work with frozen-up mechanical equipment. His fertile mind worked quickly on such matters and he rapidly was drawn into designing and fabricating electrically heated mounts for range-finders and other instruments. This, in turn, led to his being given access to restricted areas and to an increasing amount of top secret information. From the dead-lines he was given for the designing and fitting of certain items, it was easy to work out which tide a particular ship would sail on. The specifications for each job gave a clear indication of whether a ship was departing on an Arctic or an Atlantic convoy. The result was that his reports were increasingly becoming forecasts, rather than a record of past convoys.

Chapter 24

Towards the end of 1941, the progress of the war took a most unexpected and dramatic turn. David had turned in early on the night of the 7th of December. However, he was up, dressed and down for breakfast before 7am on the 8th. There he found an astonished group of naval officers all seemingly speaking at once. At last he singled out one to get the news.

"It's the Japs! They've attacked the American fleet in Pearl Harbour! Sunk dozens of their ships at anchor! The United States are now at war with the Japs! What'll happen in Europe now is anyone's guess! The Japanese have simultaneously attacked Malaya. Now Britain and America are all in it together."

"That's terrible," said David. "This has got to be a major set-back for us. We've more than enough on our plate in Europe and Africa without the problems of another enemy the other side of the world. Besides, think of the threat to our raw materials!"

"Yeah! Rubber, copper and goodness knows what else. And at this point, there's no reason why the United States should be drawn into the war against Germany. So we've a new foe and a friend who's first priority'll be to get their own back for Pearl Harbour!

Doesn't look good."

Deeply worried, David headed off to the brassfoundry. There he sought out Jimmy Mc Duff.

"You've heard the news, I suppose?" he asked.

"Aye! That'll bring the States into the war with a vengeance!"

"Vengeance'll be the operative word. We can't expect the American people to be interested in Europe now. Their war will be fought in the Pacific. We're bound to get fewer supplies from America now and just at a time when we've a new conflict out East on our hands."

"It's certain to take some of the heat off Hitler. I can't see Roosevelt being able to get the American people to declare war on Germany. The supplies to the Russians will also decline, I imagine."

"True," said David, "and that may be no bad thing. I still fear a Russian break-through and the communists arriving at Calais in a matter of weeks. They'll not stop there!"

"You think they'll attack Britain?"

"I'm sure of it! We'll be fighting the Battle of Britain all over again, but this time against the Reds!"

. . . .

In the event, David's fears were groundless. Three days after Pearl Harbour, the Germans rather unaccountably declared war on America, thus relieving the President of any necessity to try to persuade the American people to get involved in the

European conflict. Far from slowing down the supplies of munitions to their British and Russian Allies, the United States stepped up their convoys. The massive supplies reaching Russia might have worried David were it not for the fact that, having endured an horrific Russian winter, the Germans took the initiative in the spring of 1942 and by mid summer were closing in on Moscow.

Chapter 25

The evening of the 22nd of February 1942 was bitterly cold. Arthur Nelson lay on his bed, trying to contain the storm that raged within him. It had been a bad week at work. His foreman seemed to victimise him, being hypercritical about everything Nelson had done. And his work-mates had been incessantly baiting him about his English accent. His sheer impotence to hit back at them frustrated him. Impatiently, he waited for his landlady to go off to her pub. Once she left him alone, he would show Glasgow and the Scots just how impotent he was!

Half an hour later he was able to move into action. A short tram run took him far enough from his digs. Now, crouched in the ruins of partially demolished shop in Glasgow's Pollockshaws district, Nelson watched half a dozen lads playing cowboys and Indians in the rubble the other side of the street. He shivered and pulled his coat more tightly round him. They couldn't go on playing all night, especially as the blackout made everything even darker than usual on this moonless night. Eventually they split up and moved away in twos and threes. Only one set off home on his own. Nelson moved noiselessly after him, keeping in the shadows. The boy entered a courtyard. Nelson closed in rapidly. Taking the child from behind, he wrapped his hand round the boy's mouth and dragged him into a disused wash-house he had reconnoitred earlier. He shut the heavy door behind him. With one hand still gagging the youngster, he lit the stub of a candle he had previously placed on the boiler. He then drew out his knife.

"One word and you're dead! Understand?"

The boy nodded, tears running down his cheeks. Nelson slowly removed his hand.

"Sit down there," he ordered curtly. The child did as he was told. Producing a length of strong twine from his pocket, Nelson rapidly tied the boy's hands behind his back. He thrust an oily rag in the kid's mouth and tied a cord tightly round his head to ensure that the gag stayed in position. Cautiously, he opened the door and, for a few moments peered through the darkness outside, listening for any movements. Beyond the rattle of the occasional tram on the nearby main road and the sound of escaping steam from a boiler at a neighbouring factory, there was only silence. He closed the door and swung his knife until it was just below the boy's chin. This was the point when he really felt his power. In slow, deliberate tones he started to tell the terrified kid just what he was going to do to him. Sheer naked fear built up in the boy's eyes and a tremendous surge of pleasure swept over Nelson. The child was shaking convulsively now. Nelson's whole body thrilled at the experience of wielding total power over another being. Then, disappointingly, the kid's face turned blue. There were one or two more convulsive twitches and then he was still.

Nelson felt for a pulse. Nothing! A mixture of pride and disappointment nearly overwhelmed him. This was ultimate power! He had literally scared the child to death. The only pity was that it was all over so quickly.

He checked outside the wash-house again. Quiet as a grave. He picked up his knife and stood over the little corpse. The second phase of his pleasure was only beginning! One advantage of the little wretch being dead was that the blood would not spurt on to his clothing. He started to work with his knife.

Chapter 26

Throughout the year, David continued to radio his regular reports to O'Neill. He had become quite expert at transmitting by Morse code and this in turn perhaps made him slightly careless. On the very night Arthur Nelson was doing his grisly work in Pollockshaws, David had sent an unusually lengthy report from the pattern store in Dumbarton during the early hours of a Thursday morning and had then returned to Helensburgh to catch some sleep. As he entered, he met two Naval officers who were just leaving. He knew them both well and was more than a little surprised to find them going out at 3am.

"Must dash," said one of them apologetically. "Bit of a flap on, you know. Some spy's been sending messages for weeks from somewhere upriver and the Navy's been trying to get a fix on him. Tonight they got bearings and are having a big sweep. With any luck, we'll have him in the bag by dawn."

Hiding his consternation, David asked, "How accurate a fix can you get?"

"Oh! Within a mile or so. After that it's a matter of searching every likely house or building. Everyone on the streets will be checked up on. If the agent carries his radio from one place to another, with any luck, someone will catch him red-handed. Best of all would be if he starts broadcasting again. The radio-direction finding boys will be able to narrow the field down to within a hundred yards and we'll have him. However, mustn't delay. See you later!"

David was shocked. He had not considered himself in any sense a spy, but he knew that was how his actions would be interpreted. He would now just have to trust to luck that, if the pattern store was searched, his efforts at concealing the radio were adequate.

The next few hours were worrying. David was unable to sleep, but he could not immediately return to Dumbarton without attracting attention to himself. When he did reach the foundry soon after nine in the morning, he found everything going on as usual. One of the design staff, a young fellow called John McKinley who had been working throughout the night, was just leaving. He greeted David.

"Good morning, sir. We had a bit of excitement here last night soon after you left. Lorry loads of soldiers descended on the town. Apparently there's been some sort of spy scare. Someone's been sending coded messages and they're looking for the radio. They have been searching through all sorts of premises. Even were up the church steeple! The minister was affronted! They were in here and had a snoop round. One of the intelligence chaps was pouring over the list of employees and they've been questioning any with any kind of Polish or other East European-sounding names. If I were a spy I think I'd call myself Smith or Jones or something. Certainly I would not hang on to a foreign-sounding name!"

"It's hard to see how anyone could be sending messages from here," said David. "I hope they did not hold up production too much."

"No, it wasn't too bad. I think they soon realised that this is altogether too public a place for a spy to operate from. Certainly, they didn't stay long. They may, of course, have caught him. No doubt someone here will pick up word in the pub if they did. Anyway, if they didn't catch him, they will have warned him off and he won't be transmitting from Dumbarton again!"

With that, the two parted, David in a very thoughtful mood. He would have to be extremely careful. Fortunately, he was due to leave for Blairgowrie that evening and was not due back in Dumbarton until after the week-end. He would be able to transmit a message from the cave and, after that, lie low for a few weeks. The war in Russia was approaching stale-mate. The Russians had checked the German advance but were barely holding their own. If they could hold out until winter, the Nazis would again be paralysed by the mud and the snow until the Spring of 1943. Perhaps the American and British forces would be able to invade by mid-summer.

Chapter 27

David prepared and coded a detailed message to the effect that he was lying low meanwhile and would not be transmitting from Clydeside in the near future. It did not seem very important anyway as there was no immediate prospect of a Russian breakthrough. So far as anyone could read the situation, the Russians were in no position to drive westwards. The fall of both Moscow and Stalingrad seemed imminent and, although it was generally thought that the Nazis would advance no farther that summer, there was no realistic chance of them suffering a major setback. Apart from the inevitable nervous tension as he trekked from the cottage to the cave, David thoroughly enjoyed the weekend break. If he ever were questioned on one of these trips, he would be hard pressed to explain why he found it necessary to carry a heavy motorcar battery in his ruck-sack. However, the chances of being stopped and searched were slight indeed. He had been a well-known face in the glen long before the out-break of war and the likelihood of anyone questioning him was negligible.

The most significant event of the latter part of 1942 was the Allied victory at Alamein. The British Eighth Army, superbly equipped for once and brilliantly led by the charismatic Montgomery, began to push the German army under Rommel relentlessly westwards. Meanwhile, American forces led by Eisenhower had landed in west Africa and Rommel's forces were trapped between the two. Although, in the event, it was well on into 1943 before the last German forces surrendered in North Africa, long before the end of 1942 the outcome was clear. All this was very satisfactory from David's point of view. The Allied victory in Africa was obviously only a prelude to an Allied assault on mainland Europe. The sooner this happened, the farther east the eventual frontier between capitalist Europe and communist Asia was likely to be.

As the spring of 1943 unfolded, the German offensive in Russia recommenced. At first Hitler's forces were again victorious but, as the spring gave way to summer, the tide slowly began to turn. Here and there, the German's were forced back. In Africa, by late spring the fighting was all over. Then, in early summer, the Allies landed, first in Sicily, then in Italy. Italian resistance to the Allied advanced faltered, then collapsed, and by September, Italy had surrendered.

The Allied convoys supplying the Russians had taken a terrible mauling that summer. The general public were kept in the dark, but David was able to pick up snippets of information. The losses had been so horrific that convoys were suspended over the summer months. Whilst he was naturally saddened to hear stories of individual hardship and suffering, David was by no means sorry to hear that supplies were no longer reaching the Red army. The more difficult the struggle in the east, the less the risk of a sudden Russian breakthrough.

However, by autumn, all this changed. A massive tank battle had been fought at Kursk and the Germans had lost, albeit at terrible cost to the Russians. The battle was lost, but the campaign was far from over. Bitter fighting went on around Stalingrad and for a long time it was far from clear what the likely outcome would be. The Arctic convoys began again and, as he learnt of this, David's anxieties increased. He began transmitting sporadically again, carefully detailing all that he could glean about the ships and their cargoes. He used the Dumbarton radio as little as possible, trying to make his transmissions coincide with his visits to Blairgowrie.

Chapter 28

As early as Autumn of 1942, it had become clear that Hitler was starting to lose ground. In Africa, Rommel's campaign was doomed. The onset of a second Russian winter had brought fresh suffering to both sides in the conflict there, but the Germans undoubtedly felt the hardships more than the communist forces did. The Allied bombing offensive was hitting the German heartland hard. At this stage, the dispassionate observer might begin to predict an eventual Allied victory. However, no-one could possibly foretell where the respective Allied armies might be when the fighting stopped. The Russians had fought to the point of exhaustion, at terrible cost in lives. The British and Americans seemed still far short of being ready to land in Europe in the overwhelming strength that would be essential if they were not to be thrust back into the sea by the defending Germans.

O'Neill visited Scotland again just before Christmas and the three met up again in Blairgowrie. The conversation was overshadowed by the fear that all three had of a sudden collapse of the German army in Russia and of the Red army making a dash for the channel before the British and Americans could put a single soldier ashore.

"It's madness to go on arming the Russians," exclaimed Myers. "It may have made sense a year ago, but every bullet we give them now is one less for our own forces. If we are not careful, we will suddenly find that we've been arming our enemies and that the Reds are shooting our soldiers with the very bullets we provided."

"Yes, but what on earth can we do about it at this stage," demanded David. "Any political intervention will be seen as an attempt to bolster up Hitler and the suggestion of cutting support for Stalin will be turned down flat."

"You're right, to be sure," said O'Neill. "The only thing to do is to take direct action to hinder the supplies reaching Russia. We agreed that the time might come for hard decisions and I think it's come now. We have been monitoring the shipping movements and have quite a good flow of information. You two are making a valuable contribution, but I'm also getting data from Liverpool, Belfast and Bristol. Add to that snippets from Scapa Flow, Invergordon and Rosyth on the movements of Navy ships and we can predict the times and routes of the Arctic convoys fairly accurately. The time has come to leak some of this to the German embassy in Dublin. If the convoy losses rise sharply, the Government will have to think again."

David was horrified. "You mean you're suggesting that we help the Germans? Are you mad?"

"Think of it more as hindering the Russians than helping the Germans. The Nazis are going to be defeated. The question is by whom? Who will occupy Germany? Who will occupy Poland? If the Russians have it all their own way they will be charging across Germany and France long before we're even ashore on Continental Europe!"

"Yes, I know there's a very real danger of that, but what you're suggesting is going to cost British sailors their lives! How many extra British ships will be sunk if we tell the Hun where they can be intercepted?"

O'Neill nodded. "It will cost lives. Possibly a thousand or so. But think of the alternative. If the Russians overrun Europe, it will cost half a million or more British and American lives to chase them out again. If they are not resisted by force, not only will all Continental Europe fall, but they will take over Britain and Eire as well. Again, countless British lives will be lost in the struggle. Stalin has already shown that he does not mind how many Russians die to achieve victory. He won't stop at the Channel, you can be sure of that. If we could ensure that just one convoy was really badly mauled, the Government would have to call a halt."

"I'm not at all keen on this," said Myers. "Is there no alternative strategy that would achieve the same end without the loss of British lives?"

"A limited amount of sabotage could delay the departure of individual ships with no-one being hurt, but that would not make a huge difference to the tonnage of supplies reaching Russia. All that would happen is that security would be stepped up until further sabotage became impossible. We can do what we can in that direction, but as a strategy, it will not work on its own."

Very reluctantly, the two Scots agreed that the

Irishman was right. If supplies flowed uninterrupted to the Red Army, there was a very good chance of a Russian victory within a year, with disastrous consequences for Europe. The countries suffering under Nazi occupation would simply exchange one oppressor for another. It had to be admitted that it would be hard to choose between the two as to which would be worse.

"Right" said O'Neill, "if that is agreed, it's obviously vitally important that we get as much information as quickly as possible. It means, David, that you'll need to start transmitting from Dumbarton again. I know there's some risk, but can you not shift your set from one location to another at irregular intervals so they find it impossible to get a fix on you?"

"Well, yes. I suppose I could. It will be a bit tricky sending from Helensburgh with the Navy chappies always nosing around, but I should be able to do something."

"Another thing," said O'Neill. "I've got some small gelignite charges with timers. I'll give you both some and if you do get a chance to place one, you may cause a ship to miss its convoy."

"David might," replied Stephen Myers, "but I won't. I'm never on ships and simply won't have any opportunities."

"I'm sometimes on ships, but the chance of placing a charge where it will do significant damage isn't likely to come my way." David said. "Besides, it would be easily traceable back to me."

"Well, take the charges anyway," said O'Neill. "You

never know when you might be glad to have them."

The charges were very simple and, after only an hour's instruction, David felt reasonably confident that he could use them effectively, although he was still certain he would not get a chance.

As they parted, O'Neill remarked, "I see your police have still not caught your mad knife-man."

"No," replied David. "There were another two murders last month alone. The one before those was during a bombing raid two months back. The poor youngster was hurrying to a shelter but never got there. With all the racket of sirens, bombs, anti-aircraft guns and so on, no-one saw or heard a thing. I suppose it could be someone who's been literally driven mad by the stresses of war. How the police set about finding him, I just don't know. It's really awful!"

"Funny the way he strikes at irregular intervals. I wonder if it could be a seaman whose ship puts into Glasgow every now and then?"

"Could be, I suppose. But when you're dealing with a madman, it must be very difficult for the sane to know what triggers each attack."

Chapter 29

The New Year was celebrated with more optimism at Helensburgh than the previous two New Years had been. There were only some half a dozen officers billeted in the house and it was a muted but happy occasion. David gleaned a remarkable amount of information by sympathetically listening to the men forecasting what the early days of 1943 might hold for them. As a result, he was able to transmit a detailed report on the size and timing of the next convoy. The chances of the Germans being able to intercept it seemed fairly remote, however. The Arctic night had set in and the ships, although they had to travel fairly close to the coast of northern Norway, were nearly impossible for either submarines or bombers to hit except in the very short period of twilight that passed for daylight in those latitudes.

Taking advantage of the reduced number of Navy types around his home, David managed to sling a length of copper wire between two chimneys in a position that could not be seen from the ground. One of these chimneys was for a long-disused boiler in the basement and he passed the wire down it. In the basement, among antique laundry equipment, he made a hiding place for the radio. With some difficulty, he recovered the set from the attic at Dumbarton and brought it home with no-one noticing anything amiss. There would always be a risk involved every time he moved it, but, by transporting along with other bits of machinery he was legitimately working on, he could be reasonably confident that it would be unnoticed. Much of his own design and development work was of a highly secret nature anyway, so no-one would be surprised at his taking great security precautions.

Throughout January, he sent several reports, always taking care to keep the transmission time as short as possible. To his relief, there were no more spy scares. Whether his transmissions were passing unnoticed or whether the counter-espionage people had too much else to worry about, he did not know. Early in March he transferred the radio set back to the pattern store at Dumbarton

The winter was quite severe and, although travelling to Blairgowrie by train was easy enough, the glen road was frequently blocked by snow and the cottage quite inaccessible. It was therefore nearly Easter before he next made a transmission from the cave. There had been a lot of movement on the Clyde and the ship-repair yards had been very busy patching up damaged freighters. It was obvious that a major convoy was to sail soon and David had a detailed report to give on the ships and their probable cargoes. A substantial force of Royal Navy escort ships was assembling, both in the Clyde and in the deep water sea-lochs of Torridon and Duich. It was surprisingly easy for David to soak up information of a highly secret nature without ever asking a direct question.

That Friday he went to Blairgowrie, arriving just before noon. There was a lot of work to be cleared up and it was well into the evening before he reached his bungalow. The house was cold and, although he soon had a roaring fire in the stove in the large kitchen that was doubled as both living room and bedroom on his week-end stays, the chill persisted. Late on in the evening, he slipped out the back door, wheeled out his bicycle and was soon heading swiftly and silently up the glen.

There were snow drifts still lingering here and there and, rather than cycle all the way once the road became slippy with polished snow, he hid the bicycle under a hedge and took a short cut over a ridge that brought him to his cottage. As it had an open aspect to the south, the weak spring sunshine had cleared the snow away from the front of it. Nevertheless, it was like an ice-box. Pausing only to pick up one of the heavy car batteries that the wind generator had kept fully charged, he packed it in the specially modified rucksack that he kept for carrying the batteries and strode off up the hill. It was a bitterly cold clear night. The stars shone brightly and the waning moon with a frosty halo round it provided all the light he needed to guide him up the familiar route to the cave. He arrived fully twenty minutes before he was scheduled to transmit. Pulling out a flask and some sandwiches, he gratefully used the time to eat and drink.

The report he sent was unusually long and complicated. For over an hour he was transmitting. By the time the coded message 'received and understood' came in reply, the signal was weakening. The battery had done its job, but only just. He glanced at his watch. Almost 2.30am. Making sure every trace of his presence was remove and, wiping any finger-prints off the set itself before concealing it, he then hurried back down the hill. He decided to hide the battery and pick it up at a later date. This allowed him to head direct to where his bicycle lay hidden and knocked over an hour off the time of the return journey to Blairgowrie. He reached the bicycle and was soon swishing through the night with only the moonlight to guide him. A couple of miles out of Blairgowrie, his alert ears picked up the sound of a heavy engine approaching. Rather than risk having to explain his presence, he lifted the bicycle over the dry-stone wall and hid beside it in the undergrowth. The noise grew louder and soon an army lorry packed with soldiers loomed out of the darkness. As it growled by, the sound of a second vehicle not far behind reached him. Keeping well out of sight, David watched this second lorry, then a third, a fourth and a fifth roll by. There must have been thirty men in each, a total of

perhaps 150. It was far too dark to see what sort of a unit they were. All he could really discern were the silhouettes of men and rifles.

David waited until the distant sound of the engines had died away and utter silence reigned before he emerged from his hiding place. He decided it was safer to leave the bicycle and to proceed on foot. The two mile journey passed without incident and he crept in through the back door of the bungalow. The stove had done a good job. The room was welcomingly warm and in a matter of a few minutes, he had removed his outer clothes, climbed into bed and was sound asleep.

Chapter 30

Despite the lateness of his bed-time, David was up and about early the following morning. It was vitally important that he recover his bicycle before anyone else might stumble across it. He shouldered his rucksack and set out as he had done so many times before for a day on the hills. So far as he knew, no-one noticed his departure and, half an hour later, he was pedalling up the glen road. He rounded a bend and found himself faced with a road-block manned by four men of the Homeguard. He drew up and was immediately recognised by one of them.

"Why! It's Mr Campbell! Good morning to you, sir!"

"And a good morning to you. You're up and about early today. Is this some kind of special exercise?"

"Indeed not, sir! This is the real thing! Some Jerry spy's been sending messages from somewhere up the glen. There's a couple of hundred regulars plus some of our lads combing the hills right now. Mind you, I doubt if they've much chance of getting the bandit. The area is so vast that you could lose a dozen men no bother even if they weren't trying to hide. If this cove lies low in the peat-hags, it'll only be luck if he gets caught."

"I don't fancy hiding out in the heather for any length

of time myself," replied David. "This weather would be the death of you!"

While they were talking a jeep with four uniformed men swept down the glen. An officer jumped out.

"And who have we got here?" he demanded.

"It's Mr Campbell from Glasgow, sir. He's got a cottage up the glen. He's been coming here since he was a laddie. Very well known in the glen and in Blairgowrie. He owns the big garage on the Dunkeld road."

"And what brings you up here at this time of morning, Mr Campbell?" asked the officer. "I'm surprised to see a business man like yourself here so early."

"I'm up for a spot of climbing," replied David. "This is the first week-end I've managed to get away for weeks. We've a brass foundry in Glasgow and, as you can imagine, we've been working all the hours there are! I'm glad to be able to get away once in a while. Usually this glen is a haven of peace and you can escape from the war here. It seems bit

different today, though! I gather that you've a bit of a flap on?"

"Where's this cottage of yours, then?" asked the soldier.

"A mile or two up the glen and off to the right up a farm track. I've not been up there for weeks. And to think that I used to be up here almost every week-end before the war!"

"I think we'd better have a look at it. Jump in the jeep and we'll just check it out."

In a matter of minutes, the jeep with the five men crushed in it bounced its way up to the little cottage.

"Do you think anyone could have been transmitting from here?" David asked.

"Not likely, it seems. The direction finding boffins reckon it must have been higher up the glen and that it's unlikely that a signal transmitted from the floor of the valley would have travelled very far. The main body of our force is concentrating on the buildings which are high up. All the inhabitants seem to have lived here for decades. There are no strangers in the area, which makes it all very puzzling."

The jeep pulled up outside the cottage. The soldiers positioned themselves strategically round the building and David opened the door. A quick glance round the sparsely furnished rooms satisfied the officer that there was no-one inside. Nevertheless, the soldiers began a very thorough search. Every inch was scrutinised. Even the privy round the back was searched. It was obvious that the soldiers were hunting for any sign of radio equipment. David was thankful that he had been so scrupulously careful to leave absolutely no trace of anything suspicious. The officer stopped at the accumulators.

"That's a fair amount of battery power you've got there. Why do you need all that?"

"It's for lighting," replied David. "The generator only charges when the wind blows and, in winter, we get days on end when there is no wind, just biting cold. The batteries should all be fully charged now, of course, as the lights haven't been on for weeks."

"Could anyone have used them last night?"

"It should be possible to check," replied David. "I've a hydrometer here. We can check the state of charge in each cell. If anyone has used them it'll show because there was absolutely no wind last night."

So saying, he squatted down and the two checked each cell in turn. Although he was very confident of the outcome, David could feel cold sweat trickling down his back as did the job. Every cell showed up as fully charged.

"I didn't really think it likely," said the soldier, straightening himself up. "As I said, the transmitter was traced to somewhere north of here by a few miles and it's probably well up the hill."

"If it's in the middle of one of the pine plantations it will be nearly impossible to find. The forests are dense and an aerial strung up a tree would be almost totally invisible from the ground. It could even be that there's an underground bunker somewhere up there. With all the young men off either as service men or working down south on war work, there are only the women and children and the very old men left in the glen. There will be no-one going through these plantations from one year to another." David remarked.

"I gather you know the high tops here as well as anyone. Would it be possible for a German plane to land on the plateau?"

"Not a chance! It is relatively flat up there, but there are deep boggy areas and substantial boulders sticking up. In the depths of winter, when there's been heavy snow, the tops are sometimes covered by an ice-cap which levels the place out. Even then, boulders tend to protrude. It might be possible to land a light plane with skis but I wouldn't like to try it! What you could do is to make parachute drops. An agent could set out strings of lights on the ground knowing that there would be no-one around for miles to see them. The problem would be getting men and equipment down from the plateau without being noticed."

"Well, we'll do a thorough search. May I suggest, Mr Campbell, that you do not go hill-walking north of here today. I wouldn't like you to get shot, you know!"

David smiled. "I don't fancy it myself! Perhaps I'll go back to Blairgowrie and have a hike on the hills to the west of the town. That will be well out of your way. By the way, if you want to use this cottage as a base for your operations now or later, you're welcome to it. The key's always hanging on the hook under the eaves."

"Well! Thanks very much! I think we may take you up on your offer. If we don't catch the spy today, we'll need to maintain a force here for some time and perhaps be able to close in on him while he's actually transmitting next time."

"Glad to be of help," said David. "I'll walk back and pick up my bike. I'll leave you my business card. It would be helpful if you would let me know when you're finished with the cottage." And, with that, they parted.

Chapter 31

The experiences of the week-end left David badly shaken. He did go hill-walking in the low hills north and east of Dunkeld, less because he felt like it and more because, having said he would, it might look funny if he did not. The solitude did, however, give him time to think. It was obvious that he could not use the cave transmitter for some considerable time. It might be unwise ever to venture near it again. This brought the added risk of concentrating on Dumbarton and Helensburgh. He would radio his news and see if he could be supplied with another set, although where to site this would be another headache.

He considered the option of announcing that he had run enough risks and that he was closing down his operation. There were considerable attractions to this plan. However, this was not the time to lose his nerve. There had been major publicity of a massive Soviet victory at Stalingrad. Even allowing for the inevitable exaggerations for propaganda purposes, it was plain the Germans were starting to be pushed back. The Western Allies were, if anything, stepping up the flow of supplies to the Red army. What David could not understand was why Churchill and Roosevelt could not see the problems they were storing up for themselves. If the

German army cut off in Stalingrad had not made such a determined stand, there could be little doubt that the whole German front would have collapsed and the Nazis would have been pushed back hundreds of miles. Fortunately, the trapped army in Stalingrad had made an heroic stand. This had been enormously costly in German lives, but even more so in Russian. There was now a period of relatively little movement on the German/Russian front-line as both sides regrouped and desperately sought to reinforce their position. The Arctic convoys were as important to Stalin as ever and David knew that they must be hindered until the Western Allies established a bridgehead in France. The earliest that might be would be mid-summer 1943, but even that looked increasingly doubtful.

The only thing to do was to soldier on, doing all he could do to prevent the Soviets, [the Ultimate Enemy, as David increasingly thought them to be], from pushing too far westwards. He was well placed, perhaps uniquely placed to shape the course of history and he saw that as his duty, not only to Britain, but to the whole of the free world.

In the early hours of Monday morning, David transmitted a brief message explaining his position. He was not greatly surprised when Myers turned up later that week.

"I gather you've hit some problems. O'Neill was in touch, saying you had sent some first-class material but that you might have difficulty in future."

"Too true!" David said with a wry smile. "I think I had a very narrow shave last week-end. I sent a rather long message and it seems they got a fix on it. Fortunately I did not transmit from here or I might have been caught red-handed. I can only risk sending very short messages for a while to come. It's a bit of a nuisance as I might easily have a lot to say."

"I can pass on my transmitter to you, if that would help. It will leave me out of touch for a week or two until O'Neill can replace it. Your sources are better than mine and if I think it would be best if you were the one to carry on for the time being. Can you arrange for it to be picked up in Perth?"

"That's tricky," replied David. "Petrol rationing being what it is, it is out of the question to use a car. I have been seriously wondering if I ought simply to drop out. I've run a lot of risks already and it might be wise to stop while I'm winning, so to speak."

"I can see what you're getting at, but this is not the time for any of us to lose our nerve. The most important days may lie just ahead."

"Yes, I appreciate what you're saying," replied David. "Even allowing for the inevitable exaggerations for propaganda purposes, the Soviets have undoubtedly won a major victory at Stalingrad. The Germans are starting to be pushed back. That's plain for anyone to see. It's a matter of how strongly the Russians push their advantage now that's critical."

"There's that, and also the fact that the Western Allies are, if anything, stepping up the flow of supplies to the Red army. I just do not understand why Churchill and Roosevelt cannot see the problems they're storing up for themselves.

You know, if the German army cut off in Stalingrad had not made such a determined stand, I think the whole German front might have collapsed. If that had happened, the Nazis could have been pushed back hundreds of miles by now."

"Too true!" replied David. "Stalingrad must've cost tens of thousands of German lives, but without that heroic stand, the whole of Europe might be in Russian hands in a matter of a couple of months from now."

"Well, as it happened, it cost the Reds very dearly too. Both armies are bled white at the minute, so there'll be something of a stalemate for a few weeks while they regroup. No doubt the Arctic convoys will be all the more important to Stalin. They must be hindered until the Western Allies establish a bridgehead in France. However, that may be months from now."

"Well, I suppose we'll just have to soldier on and accept that there will be some measure of risk. I'm beginning to wonder if the invasion of France will take place this year at all. It may well be into 1944 before they're ready."

"You may well be right. If so, our role is more important than ever. The Soviets are the ultimate enemy and they must be stopped at all costs. Ideally, the British and Americans should overrun Germany and liberate Poland, establishing the boundaries with Russia where they were in 1939."

"I don't think we can hope to achieve that, but it is true that the pair of us are uniquely placed to shape the course of history over the next few months."

"Aye! And we owe it, not only to Britain, but to the

whole of the free world to do our duty in this respect!"

"Well! There's the practical matter of getting your transmitter from Perth. I suppose we could risk bringing it across by train. I think if we did get it here, I would have to try to establish a base up Loch Lomond way. There's some good climbing on the hills to the west of the loch and that would provide cover for me going there from time to time. It's reasonably easy striking distance by bicycle. The biggest problem will be power. I can hardly explain carrying car batteries with me and access to mains power may be well nigh impossible."

"I may be able to help you there," replied Stephen. "An old aunt of mine has a small farm up near Luss. I can arrange for you to get a room there to use as a base. It's a bit off the beaten track and has no electricity. I expect you could soon rig up a windmill and make your own. You'll make a friend for life if you give my aunt a few electric lights around the place."

So it was arranged that the two would cycle up to Luss the next Sunday. The croft was everything that Stephen had described. It was hidden from the road that bordered the loch by a wide belt of trees. The buildings were dilapidated. The farm machinery was antiquated. Stephen's aunt seemed to scratch a living from growing potatoes and vegetables and by keeping three or four dozen chickens. David was able to negotiate for the use of a tumble-down bothy at a rent he considered reasonable and the old lady considered a fortune.

There was no difficulty in convincing old Mrs Myers that a low voltage electrical system which would give her a limited amount of light at the press of a switch was a distinct improvement on her old oil lamps. During the week that followed. David fabricated the generating system and, on a long Sunday of hard work, he set the whole thing up, together with some redundant overhead wiring between the buildings and the generator. This latter provided an excellent concealed aerial. The transmitter was still in Stephen's care, so David brought up his own one from Dumbarton, transporting it in a bulging rucksack as he pedalled up the loch-side. He stayed over that night and, in the early hours of Monday morning made a brief test transmission. Everything worked perfectly.

By nine o'clock that morning, he was cycling in through the gates at the Dumbarton foundry. In the drawing office he was greeted by Jimmy McDuff.

"Good morning, David! We had another security panic at the week-end. As you know, I'm in the Home Guard and they roped us in to search the town. Apparently our neighbourhood spy's been at it again! The detection chappies have been picking up his signals at regular irregular intervals, if you know what I mean. He keeps on transmitting, but not at a regular time, so they find it difficult to get a fix on him. Apparently the messages have been getting shorter and that's not helping."

"Good gracious!" David exclaimed. "Did you catch him?"

"No such luck!" was the reply. "They had us searching all through Sunday. They've been all through the yard here. They were hoping to trace the transmitter by using metal-detectors. You know, those new-fangled things they use to hunt for land-mines. No chance here where practically everything's made of metal. I'm sorry, but they even searched your office. I tried to stop them but the Captain insisted."

"That's perfectly all right," said David. "It's important that every possibility be eliminated. Did they think the transmissions were coming from somewhere close to here, then?"

"Well, that's what they thought. They'd been picking them up from the other side of the river from two separate points and they reckoned the fixes coincided somewhere here or hereabouts. Then, just as we were all winding up the search, the phone rings. It was the detector unit on the south side. The spy had sent a short burst and it looks as though the earlier one was wrong. This one seemed to be coming from some distance north of here."

"Couldn't your friend be carrying his transmitter in a vehicle and sending from various places? That would explain why it's so hard to pin him down."

"Someone suggested that. It is possible. However, he would have to run the risk of being stopped at a random road-block and perhaps being searched. These radios are quite bulky and they would be hard to hide. I'm not convinced the direction finding is all that reliable. Probably the guy's hidden away in some tenement or even a bombed out building. I was speaking to the 'Sparks' on one of the freighters and he reckons that the radio waves don't necessarily travel in the same straight line all the time, depending on atmospheric conditions. If that's remotely true, direction-finding is bound to be a bit hit and miss."

David thought for a minute. "The inaccuracy is going to vary with the distance you are from the transmitter, if that's the case. If you could set up your equipment really close to the radio set, you should be able to pin-point the source fairly accurately."

"That's what I said! I suggested that they monitor the town for a week, with detection gear concealed at suitable points. The expert said that, in a town this size, the spy would get wind of their presence and simply wouldn't send."

"I'd have thought they could be a bit more discreet than that!" exclaimed David. "If you wanted, they could set up somewhere in the buildings here, the pattern store, for instance. If you and I brought in a load of drawings from Blairgowrie, the detection stuff could be smuggled in with it and only the two of us would know. It's not that I think for one moment that there's a spy on the payroll, but those who didn't know anything couldn't accidentally give the show away. What do you think? Is it worth suggesting? I'll leave it with you. You know I'll co-operate with anything that looks as though it might trace this fellow."

"Well! Thank you! I'll certainly suggest it."

"I'd better get started on my real work now that we've done our spy-catching for the day!" David said with a grin, and he entered his own office, closing the door behind him. As he did so, the smile faded and became a worried frown. They were getting too close for comfort. He would have to cover his tracks even more carefully in future.

Chapter 32

It so happened that there was little to report over the next week or so. David went to Blairgowrie for a couple of days, stopping off in Perth on the way for a pre-arranged conference with Myers. The upshot was that Myers undertook to send a brief report explaining David's radio silence. They agreed that the transfer of the other radio to the west was too risky at present. Although it would delay messages by a day or so, they arranged that David would contact Stephen whenever there was something really significant to report and then Myers would transmit it. As things worked out, however, there was little to send. There was tremendous shipping activity on the Clyde, almost all to do with the Atlantic convoys. Every week or so one of the giant Cunard liners, either the Queen Mary or the Queen Elizabeth, would arrive, its decks teeming with American soldiers. Obviously, the Allied forces were being built up ready for the impending invasion of Europe. David reported nothing of this. His mission was concerned only with the supply of armaments for the Russians.

The radio direction-finding equipment was duly set up in the pattern store and a twenty-four hour watch kept. The only flutter of excitement came when Stephen, on a flying visit to his aunt, sent on one of David's reports. David himself was on the premises at the time. A happy coincidence, he thought. If anyone had entertained the slightest suspicions about him, this would scotch them.

The absence of transmissions from the Clyde valley, plus the one short burst from Luss convinced the detection squad that they were wasting their time. The equipment was dismantled and things returned to normal.

As the Summer of 1943 gave way to Autumn, it became clear that there would be no invasion that year. This was worrying. The Germans were putting up ferocious resistance in the east and the Russians were paying dearly for every yard of land they gained. However, they were gaining. The front-line was definitely being pushed westwards. Every so often, the Red army would suffer a serious reverse, but it would come back with renewed vigour and strike hard at the invader. September saw a sequence of Soviet victories all along the front. However, their offensive seemed to run out of steam and for two months the fighting see-sawed one way and another. Eventually, in December, the Red army began a slow but apparently unstoppable advance, squeezing the Nazis out all along the front. Even making all the allowances he could for the British Government exaggerating the Soviet successes, David was seriously worried. There was no chance of the Western Allies landing in France before Easter and the communists might have swept all before them by then. The Arctic convoys were larger than ever, with the American liberty ships bringing vast quantities of munitions, guns and tanks, as well as food stuffs. The quantities involved were, of course, a closely guarded secret, but any one in David's position could deduce that they were enormous.

Chapter 33

Throughout the winter and on into the spring of 1943, Arthur Nelson maintained his one-man reign of terror. The teeming slums of Glasgow, plus the blackout, made this easy for him. Two more youngsters fell victim to his knife just before Easter. His technique was steadily improving. He would make a competent surgeon, he wryly told himself! But after those two, he had to call a halt. With British Double Summertime now in force, the clocks having been put forward by two hours, darkness did not fall until nearly midnight. Nelson reluctantly decided that he would have to cease operations until the autumn, despite a terrible build-up of frustration within him which was nearly more than his rational side could control. A seething mass of pent-up perverted desire, he stalked the streets of the slum areas, planning his next winter's campaign. It was clear that the children had been told to stay in large groups and, furthermore, when they were playing, there was always some woman, usually of the grand-mother age-group, discreetly keeping an eye on them.

This increased vigilance was going to be a problem, even when the dark nights returned. Nelson's solution was to go farther afield. On his days off, he explored Paisley,

Hamilton, Motherwell and several of the other towns surrounding Glasgow. The opportunities were certainly there. Come the autumn, he would branch out!

. . . .

The latter months of 1943 and the early part of 1944 was a time of great suspense. Everybody on both sides of the on-going conflict knew that the American and British armies would invade continental Europe. The unanswered questions were 'when' and 'where'. The struggle in the east continued, but it was becoming increasingly obvious that the tide had finally turned against Hitler. On every part of the front his troops were retreating, although they put up the most tremendous resistance.

David transmitted what data he could glean, but his messages were becoming shorter. With convoys assembling off Iceland and ships sailing direct from the United States to Murmansk and Archangel, the two largest Russian Arctic ports, it was difficult to get accurate information. Increasingly, he began to feel his work was over. Whether he had made the significant difference he had hoped for, only time would tell. The Spring came, but still the Western Allies did not invade. The German 'V1's', nick-named 'doodlebugs', started to rain down on the south-east of England. The Nazis were certainly not out of the game yet, although few entertained serious doubts about an eventual defeat for the Germans.

There had been no heavy raids on Glasgow and the towns along the Clyde for over a year and the general feeling was that in that respect the worst was over. However, fear still gripped the community. As the days shortened in the late autumn of 1943, the mad knife man started killing again. Throughout the winter, children disappeared. Then their mutilated bodies would turn up. The killer was ranging more widely, his attacks mainly being in the centre of the city and in those satellite towns to the east, south and west. Mercifully, the towns on the northern bank of the Clyde escaped his attentions. Only when the long hours of daylight came in May of 1944 did the murders stop, eventually raising the question in the minds of many by mid-summer that the man responsible might be in the forces and now be in France. He was not. Nelson was once again closing down operations for the duration of double summer time.

During the spring, Nelson began to wonder if he should not seek to move from central Glasgow. The teasing of his work-mates continued unabated. He could put up with that, but when some wag pointed out that the child-killings coincided with Nelson's days off, he began to feel insecure. When he got the chance, he would quietly move on. He also wondered if he could arrange another change of name. He had almost completely stopped thinking of himself as Arthur Nelson, so comfortable was he with the identity he had taken over that night back in Bromley. If he found a chance to do another switch, he would.

. . . .

At least it seemed that Clydeside had seen the last of the German bombers. However, there was still suffering ahead.

David was returning to the foundry one evening, when a tremendous blast blew him off his feet. Winded, he struggled to rise, blood streaming down his face where flying glass had lacerated him. He staggered through the gates and gazed in horror at a gigantic crater in the yard. Most of the office block had been damaged and survivors were crawling out of the wreckage. Some were obviously badly injured. One or two lay motionless, whether dead or merely unconscious David could not tell. He realised that, although he himself was badly shaken, he had escaped serious injury. Blood was running into his eyes, temporarily blinding him.

Men were running from the other buildings, some with fire-extinguishers, some tearing at the debris with their bare hands to extricate their colleagues who were still trapped in the offices. In the distance, David could hear the clang of the bells of approaching fire-engines. He tried to run across to help but tripped and fell. When he tried to get up, his legs felt like jelly. He forced himself to his feet and promptly fainted.

Some time later, David awoke. He was so heavily bandaged, he could hardly see. His whole frame ached. The nurses in the ward were bustling around and there was an atmosphere of controlled panic as one patient after another was wheeled in and helped into bed. David shut his eyes and drifted off into something between sleep and a coma.

It was dark when he woke. He could just make out the forms of nurses going about their duties. He managed to attract the attention of one of them.

"What happened?" he asked.

"Nobody really knows, but they think it must have

been a delayed action bomb. Probably one of those dropped in the 1941 raids. Why it should suddenly go off is beyond me. However, you're not too badly hurt. A few cuts and bruises. Mind you, you'll be sore for a few days yet, but we'll soon have you as good as new." She smiled and went away.

Chapter 34

"Visitor for you, Mr Campbell!"

The nurse smiled at David as he struggled into wakefulness. It was broad daylight. In spite of his aches and pains, he had slept quite well. He looked up. His visitor was Andrew McCabe, the leading draughtsman at the foundry.

"How are you, sir?" McCabe asked. "I gather you had a close call yesterday."

"Not too bad, thanks," replied David, hitching himself up into a sitting position. "What's the story. I remember seeing two or three who looked as though they had really copped it. How bad is it?"

"Bad enough, though it could have been worse. I'm sorry, but Jimmy McDuff's gone. So is Graeme Miller, Robert McBeth and Hamish Stewart. They caught the full force of the blast and were killed outright. The only consolation is that I don't suppose they felt a thing. Harry McGregor's badly smashed up. It's touch and go whether he'll make it. Timothy Barclay's pretty bad too, but he's not in any immediate danger. He's a young, strong fellow and I've no doubt he'll pull through but it'll be a long time before he works again. There's another half dozen like yourself. You know, cuts, bruises, but nothing that won't mend soon enough."

"The nurse said it was an unexploded bomb from the raids way back. Is that so?"

"Aye. The bomb-disposal people reckon it was a land-mine that failed to go off and that it has lain there undetected ever since. Apparently that can happen. Then, for some unknown reason, it decided to explode. It's tough on the four who died and on the injured, but it could have been so much worse. Imagine if it had gone off at a change of shift, with all the chaps milling around clocking on and clocking off! It doesn't bear thinking about!"

"True," said David, "and I've much to be grateful for as well. If I'd been half a minute earlier, I'd have been blown to bits! As it is, I'll be out of here in a day or so. We're going to miss the dead and injured. It's so hard to get decent staff and, with so much work on, we're bound to have problems."

"I've applied for more men and the employment people have said they will see what they can do. As you say, at this stage of the war, it's so difficult. So many good men are in the forces and the work-force all along the Clyde is declining, what with retirements and deaths exceeding recruitment for four years now. However, we've pulled through in the past and I dare say we'll do so again."

"That's the spirit! I'll get myself out of here just as fast as I can and we'll see what sort of replacements we can lay our hands on. Thanks for coming and thanks for all the efforts you're making."

"No thanks needed, sir. I'm just so glad you escaped so lightly. It'll be great to have you back. I'd better get going now. You look after yourself and we'll see you soon."

And with that he left. David lay miserably thinking about the dead and the injured. The death of Jimmy McDuff was a severe blow. Jimmy had been the nearest thing David had had to a close friend. The other casualties he also grieved over. David was a distant, almost aloof figure to his staff but, for all that, he knew each one and had a kind of old-fashioned paternalistic care for them. The men that were gone would be a great loss and it sounded as if the two who were most seriously injured would be out of the game for a long time. The sooner he got back to work himself, the better.

Chapter 34

The very day David left hospital, the news came that the Allied forces had landed in strength in Normandy. The whole country held its breath. The first twenty-four hours were vital. Would the Allies secure a bridgehead, or would they be pushed back into the sea. And what would the price of victory be? How long would the casualty lists be? David wondered wryly whether his discharge from hospital was in order to leave as many beds vacant as possible.

The day slipped by and it was clear that, after heavy fighting and a determined defence by the Germans, the Allies were in France to stay. However long it might take, the Nazis were going to be pushed back and back, sandwiched between the Western Allies and the advancing Soviet armies. There was a decreasing amount of data on the Arctic convoys and, for all practical purposes, David shut down his operation. Whatever good he had done was now in the past. History would show if it had been sufficient to prevent a communist take-over of Europe. The American and British governments seemed at last to be alive to the issue and the combined armies of both countries were thrusting forward in a race for Berlin. In late 1944, it was impossible to guess if the Russians or the Western Allies would be there first.

. . . .

In September, as the days shortened, Nelson was once again feeling restive. The enormous sense of power and importance that had buoyed him up six months earlier when his exploits dominated the Scottish press had evaporated. No longer was he the man who made all Glasgow shiver with fear. He was once again just the outsider, the Englishman with the middle-class accent that so alienated the rest of the staff. He decided to use the cover of one of the infrequent air-raids to let the city know he was very much alive. When the sirens went, he dashed from his flat and down to the waste-ground several hundred yards away where the kids played. In the growing darkness, he caught sight of a girl of about eleven, running towards the distant communal shelter. With a kind of reckless courage, he headed her off. The sky now throbbed with air-craft and the anti-aircraft guns added their contribution to a bedlam of noise. Shouting to her as he closed the gap between them, he ordered her to take cover in a narrow alleyway between two derelict buildings. The noise reached a climax as the first bombers dropped their deadly cargo. The terrified child dashed into the alleyway for shelter, only to find she faced a new horror as Nelson bundled her into a doorway and drew his knife.

"You there! Drop that knife!"

Nelson swung round to find himself faced by two determined policemen. He seized the child and threw her bodily at the men. Then he crashed out past them, sending them sprawling. Gaining a start of a mere twenty yards, he hared off down the street as the policemen scrambled to their feet. He swung round a corner just as a stick of bombs fell.

The blast lifted him bodily, throwing him right across the road, a fact that saved his life as the building he had been passing collapsed in rubble around him. Bruised and shaken, he hauled himself erect and staggered back to the alleyway. One of the policemen was clearly dead, as was the child. The second constable was very much alive but his legs were pinned under a heavy beam. Nelson clambered over the wreckage until he was behind the prostrate man. He picked up a large chunk of masonry and pounded the other's head flat.

As the dust began to settle, Nelson peered through the gloom. There was not a soul in sight. He shambled off down the street towards a bombed building that was burning furiously. There he allowed himself to be found in a dazed state by firemen who immediately arranged for his transfer to hospital. There, lying in the ward, he reflected on his narrow shave. He recognised that his luck was running out and so decided that, as soon as he was fit, he would move to somewhere down the river. There was a desperate shortage of skilled men and getting an engineering job in one of the ship-yards would be simple.

. . . .

David concentrated on his work. In the days following his discharge from hospital, he worked long hours. The replacements for the staff he had lost were of indifferent quality, a fact that contributed to the growth of his already excessive work-load. It was not until late autumn before he recruited a reasonably competent replacement for the muchmisssed Jimmy McDuff. The fellow, a man in his late thirties named David Hamilton, showed real promise. Hamilton was an Englishman who had been working in Scotland for some years. He had only been involved in foundry work since being drafted into munitions production after being discharged on medical grounds from the artillery in 1940. For all that, he was a very skilful engineer who could operate a variety of machines. He showed a reluctance to talk about his previous experience and, when it was learnt that he had lost his entire family in a bombing raid on Croydon and had never really got over the shock, no-one pressed him for more information.

David continued to follow the progress of the respective Allied armies with the greatest interest. As 1944 came to a close, the eventual defeat of the Nazis was clear to all. Why they did not throw in the towel, particularly on the western front, David could not understand. Their fanatical resistance was bleeding their forces to death. The civilian population were suffering terribly. Whilst they could expect no mercy from the Russians, some accommodation with the Western Allies surely should have been sought, if only to bring the war to an end while the Russians were on Polish, rather than German, soil. But no! Hitler fought on with a maniacal tenacity. Every yard was contested and it was not until April that the Russians entered Berlin. Even then, the defeated capital was fought for street by street and house by house. Eventually the inevitable happened. Unable to fight any longer, the Germans surrendered, Hitler killed himself and the war in Europe ended.

A month or so before the end of hostilities, the Navy decided they no longer needed David's Helensburgh home. It took a little adjusting to the fact that he no longer shared the house with a variety of strangers. At first he had resented their presence and the resultant lack of privacy in his own home, but now they were gone, he found the house almost oppressively quiet. He soon got used to it and came to regard the changed situation as a welcome sign of a return to peace-time normality.

He was therefore alone when, one evening late in May, Stephen Myers dropped in unexpectedly. David found one of the few bottles of wine he had hoarded from pre-war days and the two sat in the bay window looking out at the sunset over the water far below them.

"I've really come to say 'good-bye' David. I'm going to disappear and we won't be seeing each other again."

"What do you mean 'disappear'," asked David.

"Well, now the Russians have taken Berlin, I'm not going to take the risk of them finding some reference to us in Nazi documents. You know what the Germans are like. Great on organisation and methods! My fear is that they kept detailed records of every despatch we sent. If I could only be sure they would be as thorough in destroying all such things as the Red Army approached, I wouldn't worry. If there are records and the communists get them, they'll pass anything like that on to MI5 and then it'll be all up with us."

"But we were radioing O'Neill in Eire," David protested. "We weren't radioing Berlin!"

"Aye! That's what I thought too. It turns out that

O'Neill is a Nazi spy. You and I were duped by him. He is an Irishman, all right, but one with a pathological hatred for England and the English. He's been passing on everything to the Germans and I'm sure they have a fat dossier on both of us. It may or may not still exist. Anyway, I'm taking no chances. I've managed to fix up a new identity and I'm just going to vanish."

"Where will you go?" David asked, suddenly very alarmed.

"Better you don't know. What you don't know, you can't let slip. It'll be better for both of us that way. It's a pity this is how it's worked out. I still think we did a good job, though. The British only just managed to reach the Baltic before the cease-fire. If the Russians had been a mere fifty miles farther on they would have cut off Denmark. Fifty miles is not a lot, when you think that they had already driven the Germans back a thousand miles and more. If they had cut off Denmark, they would've gone on to 'liberate' both it and Norway. Once they were in, the Danes and the Norwegians would never have got them out. That would leave Sweden and Finland totally isolated from free Europe. It would only be a matter of time before they fell. No! I've no regrets. No-one will understand, but we did what was right."

"That leaves me here, wondering when and if there'll suddenly be a knock at the door, then?"

"Well, you'll just have to decide whether to take your chances. Any records may have been burnt by the Nazis, if they had time. They may have been destroyed in the final battle for Berlin. After all, most of the city was left a pile of rubble. There is, however, a chance that they have survived. If the Reds get them and see we made a determined effort to undermine them, they'll make sure the British authorities get all the evidence. It's a risk I'm not prepared to take. I saw O'Neill in March. Not that he was any help. He said it was now a matter of every man for himself. And he had the nerve to give me half a dozen cyanide capsules. Look! Here they are! Said I could always take one if I didn't feel like carrying on! Some help he was! Anyway, I've managed to fix up a new identity and I'm off. I advise you to give the matter a bit of thought, although you've so much more to leave behind if you do slip away."

He slapped the phial of capsules on the coffee table. David was speechless. He had willingly taken risks that could have cost him his life, but now, when it was all over, the thought of living in daily fear of arrest, trial and execution was intolerable. He stammered his farewells and wished Myers the best of luck. Then he slumped back in his chair.

The evening became night and he still sat, motionless. What could he do? How long did he have? When might the blow fall? He wondered if he should disappear. But how? Certainly, now the war in Europe was over, life was returning to some semblance of normality, but how could you get by without a ration-book, an identity card and, most importantly, an income? There was money enough for him in America, but how could he get it without being traced? In the early hours of the morning, he gave up and went to bed.

Sleep eluded him. He lay in a cold sweat. Would they shoot him? No, it was spies they shot. He would be hanged as a traitor. Eventually, about six o'clock, realising that he wasn't going to get any sleep that night, he got up and dressed. The morning light was filtering in through the bay window where Myers and he had sat the previous evening. It caught the small phial that Myers had contemptuously pulled from his pocket. Had Myers simply forgotten to pick them up? Or had he deliberately left them? David had no way of telling. He picked the phial up and put it in a cupboard. There was no way he was going to take that way out, he thought. For all that, he did not destroy them.

He sat drinking one cup of coffee after another. Slowly, his more rational self took over. There was a real risk that incriminating records had survived. There was a real risk the Russians would find them. It was certain they would seek vengeance on any who had conspired against them. But Berlin was still in chaos. It would take weeks, if not months, for the communists to sift through whatever data they had captured intact. David realised he had time. How much was anyone's guess, but the chances of being arrested in the immediate future were reasonably remote.

He would look for a way to disappear. How one acquired a new identity without being, on the one hand, putting one's future in the hands of criminals who might at any time sell one to the authorities or, on the other hand, becoming a potential target for blackmail, he did not know. Meanwhile, he would inconspicuously accumulate as much cash as possible. He would have to leave all his real wealth behind, his businesses and his houses. He realised that and considered it would be impossible to start selling anything very significant without attracting attention to himself.

Chapter 36

The next few days were difficult. David found it hard to conceal his anxiety. At work, he tried to carry on as normal, but had problems concentrating. He took the opportunity to visit Luss for a long week-end. The freedom of the open hills lifted his spirits. With him he took the radio set from Helensburgh and, finding a cliff which overlooked a deep pool, he disposed of both sets. That was one less complication, although it would not make much difference if, with Teutonic efficiency, the Nazis had kept detailed records of all the messages he had transmitted over the years.

The war with Japan ended as unexpectedly as it had begun. The near-total destruction of Hiroshima and Nagasaki by atomic bombs forced the Japanese to surrender. The pressure of work was easing. This was a mixed blessing for David. When he was very busy, he had little time for worrying. Now, as time was slipping by, he found it harder and harder to sleep. When he did sleep, his rest was shattered by dreams of policemen, of judges and of hangmen.

David Hamilton came into his office to see him one evening.

"I'm sorry, sir, but I've come to hand in my notice. I've enjoyed working here, but I have to face up to the fact that coming to Scotland was just running away from reality. If I'm to pick up the threads of my life again, I must go back and face Croydon."

"We'll be sorry to lose you," said David very sincerely. "You came at a very difficult time for us and I do appreciate the way you've worked. I will find it hard to replace you, although work is easing off and we should soon be getting men who've been demobbed coming on to the labour market soon."

"I hope you don't feel I'm letting you down, going like this, but I really feel I must make a move or I'll never get over all that's happened in the past."

"I do understand and I do sympathise," said David generously. "For selfish reasons, I'd like you to stay, but if that's how you feel, you had better go. If you ever change your mind, there'll be a job waiting for you here."

"Thank you very much, sir. I don't want to leave you in the lurch, but, if it's all right with you, I'll work until a week on Friday. That's the last day of the month so I'll give up my digs that morning and go south on the night train."

"Well, as I say, I'll be sorry to see you go. Make sure you pop in and say good-bye on the Friday."

Chapter 37

Hamilton did drop in to say his farewells. David was alone in the office at the time. With the fall-off in work, there were no office staff working in the evening and night working had stopped. The back-shift would be there until 11pm, after which the foundry was closed for the week-end.

"Hullo, there, Hamilton!" David greeted his visitor. "My, you look terrible! Are you well enough?"

"I've caught a touch of 'flu, I think. I keep on shivering and I ache all over. The rotten thing is that I've given up my digs, so I've really got to go. Don't worry, I'll be all right."

"Nonsense, man!" David exclaimed. "You're not fit to travel. You've got to treat 'flu seriously or it'll literally be the death of you. Sling your bag into my car. I'll put you up for the night and you can go south tomorrow if you're feeling up to it"

"Really, sir, I can't put you to all this trouble. I'll be fine on the train!"

"No! I won't hear of it! Besides it's no trouble. I've put up half the Navy over the past five years! I've plenty of room. You do what you're told and I'll lock up here."

Twenty minutes later, David was helping Hamilton

up the stairs in Helensburgh. The man was really ill. Although it was a warm night and really quite hot in the house, Hamilton was shivering convulsively. He was deathly pale and looked as though he might pass out any minute. David helped him out of his outer clothes and Hamilton slumped on the bed.

"Hang on a minute," said David. "I'll go and get you a hot drink and some aspirin."

He left the room, slipping out of his jacket as he did so. He hung it on the banister at the top of the stairs before going down to the kitchen. There he put the kettle on and went down to the cellar where he knew he had a bottle of rum that one of the naval officers had given him.

While he was away, Hamilton stirred. He sat up shakily. This illness could hardly have come at a worse time. He could not stay here more than one night, but he had nowhere to go. Furthermore he very little money. Groggily, he looked round him The boss's jacket was hanging at the stairhead just outside the bedroom. Even at this range, Hamilton could see a fat wallet protruding from the inside pocket. Campbell would never miss a tenner or so. He pulled himself out of the bed. Steadying himself by leaning against the wall he shuffled out to the top of the banisters. He eased the wallet out and, sure enough, there was a substantial wad of notes. He drew several out, but, even as he did so, he heard David open the kitchen door below and then his approaching footsteps. Hamilton tried to hurry, but, as he turned, everything went black and he collapsed down the flight of stairs, fetching up with a terrible crunch against the bottom skirting-board.

Pausing only to put the tray he was carrying down, David dashed forward. He took the man's arm. It fell limply from his grasp. He felt for a pulse, but as he did so, he saw the angle of the other's neck and realised that Hamilton's troubles were over. It did not take the skills of an orthopaedic surgeon to diagnose a broken neck. David reeled back with shock. Then, slowly, he realised that, with any luck, he now had the answer to his own problems.

The first thing David did was to check the dead man's papers. Ration book, identity card and even a passport, although this was out of date. Everything he needed! Working quickly, he stripped the corpse and dressed the dead man in his clothes. He took his own wallet, complete with driving licence and identity card and slipped it in the breast-pocket. Very reluctantly, he slipped his expensive watch off his wrist and put it on Hamilton's. It was fortunate that the two were of a sufficiently similar build. He stood back and surveyed his handiwork. It would pass muster.

David had left the car at the secluded back door and, with some considerable effort he placed the body in the boot. He locked up and drove with the greatest of care back to Dumbarton. The last thing he wanted was to attract the attention of the constabulary. Once there, he locked the car and went into the foundry. Andrew McCabe was supervising the closing down of the place for the week-end.

"I'm back to finish a design I was working on," said David. "You wind up here and lock up. I'll be in the office for an hour or so. You can leave the locking up of the office block and the main gate to me."

"Can I assist you with anything?" McCabe asked helpfully. "I'm in no hurry tonight. Indeed, I'm finding it difficult to adjust to not working all the hours there are!"

"Thanks, but no. I'll manage this fine on my own. But I know what you mean, it's really quite ridiculous me being back working during the night, but it's hard to shake off the habit. No! It's just a silly little job I want to finish and have ready for Monday. I'll do it now. Then I can go hill-climbing tomorrow with a clear conscience," said David with a grin.

"Well, if you're sure. You know I'll willingly stay."

"No, I'll be fine. Off you go."

They exchanged 'goodnights' and McCabe followed the departing staff out through the foundry gate. David went into his office and pulled out various drawings which he spread across his desk. His nerves were on edge, but he had to delay for an hour or so to ensure that McCabe did not return. Just after mid-night, he extinguished most of the lights. Silently, he slipped out of the building and opened the boot of his car. With a wave of nausea sweeping through him, he lifted the inert body and dragged rather than carried it into his office. He placed it as best he could on the chair close to one of the walls. Then he opened his personal safe. Carefully he took out the gelignite charges and timers he had got so long ago from O'Neill. He bunched the charges together under the desk. Thirty minutes would be ample. He set the timer and, pausing only to pick up a suitcase of clothes he had packed from the car, he cautiously left the building and disappeared into the night. Another unexploded bomb was going to rock the yard and destroy most of the remaining office buildings. Tragically, David Campbell, the managing director, working late on his own, would be killed in the blast. With any luck the dead man's head would be blown to pieces, so even if anyone wished to try to check his identity, the dental evidence simply wouldn't be there.

Chapter 38

Five months and more had passed since the explosion at Jayemcee's Foundry in Dumbarton. David Campbell, or David Hamilton, as he was learning to think of himself as being, had read the newspaper reports. It was quite touching to read of how highly he was thought of and of how much he would be missed.

It appeared he had made his escape only just in time, however. The national press had carried two or three items about the police seeking one Stephen Myers who they thought "would be able to help them in their enquiries about a security matter." No doubt, but for the exposion at Jayemcee's offices, they would also be seeking him.

However, David was now living quietly in Liverpool. He had had no difficulty getting employment with a textile machinery manufacturer who was switching his plant from torpedo manufacture back to making looms. After only two months at his new employers, David had been asked to transfer to sales. Before the war, the company had exported widely, particularly to North America and they were anxious to re-establish their markets there. Would David be willing to travel? Yes! Anything to help the company. Would he go to Canada? Of course! Not so good as the United States, but definitely heading in the right direction. The export drive was on. A Britain which had bankrupted itself fighting for its freedom must earn foreign currency, particularly dollars. David had applied for a new passport under the name David Hamilton and his employer was trying to pull strings to get one for him. Once he reached Canada, crossing to the States should be quite easy and then he would have access to more than adequate funds. Things were really going his way!

One Thursday, he returned to his lodgings. His landlady was at the door as he came in.

"Couple of gentlemen to see you, Mr Hamilton. They're waiting in the parlour." And, with that she pushed open the door. Even if David had thought of making a dash, her ample bulk adequately blocked his exit. He entered and found two hefty men in civilian clothes waiting for him.

"David Hamilton?" asked the older of the two.

"Yes," replied David, trying to look relaxed. "What can I do for you?" Out of the corner of his eye, he saw the other man position himself between David and the door.

"Inspector Peter Goddard, and this is Sergeant Patrick Freeman, Bromley CID. Now, I think we should end this charade here and now. You're no more David Hamilton than I am!"

David gritted his teeth just in time to stop his jaw dropping. How could they have got on to him? There was not a hint in the press that David Campbell's death was regarded as anything other than a tragic result of war. Besides, where did Bromley come into it? These questions were racing through his mind when the heavily-built Goddard stepped forward and unaccountably stamped on David's right foot.

"Ouch! What the devil did you do that for?"

"David Hamilton wouldn't have felt a thing," said the big man mildly. "He lost his right foot when he was evacuated from Dunkirk. We've come from The Larches in Brockley Avenue, Bromley. It's being rebuilt and the workmen called us in when they found a corpse in the cellar, a corpse with an amputated foot. David Hamilton's corpse."

David's jaw did drop now. He blustered, "I'm not at liberty to tell you who I am or why I've adopted Hamilton's identity. I'll have to get clearance from MI6 before I can say anything."

"That won't wash and you know it! We know perfectly well who you are. The body of the man you're impersonating was found in the cellar of your uncle's house. I'm only sorry that Inspector Burnett who was so hot on your heels after you murdered those kids can't be here to arrest you. The poor fellow died in a raid in '42. However, we've got you now."

He turned and faced David. "Arthur Donald Nelson, I'm arresting you for the murder of David James Hamilton. You do not have to say..... Oh, blast! The fellow's fainted! Get the cuffs on him, Freeman, and put him in the car. Remember those poor kids, in case you're tempted to be excessively gentle with him. We'll finish the caution when he comes to and, with any luck we'll add the other charges as well."

Epilogue

The man who the police, the judicial system, the warders and the public hangman all knew as Arthur Donald Nelson sat miserably cradling his head in his hands as the last ten minutes of his life ticked away. Throughout the police interrogation and the trial, David McKay Campbell had exercised his right to remain silent. There was nothing he could have said to escape the gallows. He had been repeatedly grilled about the murder of three children in England and, with a sickening jolt, he made the connection with the wave of similar killings in Glasgow. Mercifully, the police failed to suspect him for those.

At least the reputation of the Campbell family had come through all these horrible experiences unscathed. Now he would take his secret to the unmarked grave that was already dug in the prison yard. Throughout the days awaiting trial and then the even more awful days awaiting execution, David thought longingly of the phial of poison capsules he had left in Helensburgh. From the mists of the past came the words of the kindly, grey-haired army chaplain all those years ago.

"David. Let me speak very frankly to you. You've suffered so much. These past few years have been incredibly hard for you. But you have a life ahead of you. If you face it embittered, you'll be miserable all your days. If you harbour evil thoughts against others it'll be like a cancer growing inside you. One day it'll destroy you.......

David, laddie! I'm scared for you. Please think over what I've tried to say. I know it's desperately hard, but try to let go of the past. Don't let it ruin your future happiness."

At eight on the dot the door opened and three men entered. With wordless efficiency, the few paces to the hanging shed were traversed, the noose adjusted, the lever pulled, the trap opened and the prisoner's lifeless body swung gently at the end of the rope.

Villain or Victim?